QUANTUM RAPTURE

James True

ISBN:
ISBN-13:

Dedicated to
Everett O'Neal

He showed me the world one cathedral at a time. No one has done more to teach me the power of a voice.

Contents

CHAPTER ONE

Hardy's Hand

A grimoire is a book of magic. Hardy's grimoire was written in the computer language of Perl. Every operating system has a Perl interpreter somewhere in its crevices. This made Hardy a very portable magician. Every program is someone's will echoed in their incantation. Computer spells take on a life of their own. They are given consciousness by the central processor every clock cycle. They have a finite life to do what they can with what they are given. These spells are daemons or ghosts in the machine. Daemons have urges and fight for priority over the computer's resources. Hardy's daemons have been thriving across the internet for twelve years now. He has no way of tracking all of his children. To do so would compromise their hiding places. Hardy codes in packets that yearn to survive in the loops of bounced mail autoresponders. Hardy's code hides in the bureaucracy of javascript routines embedded in a corporate site's privacy policy page. No one scrutinizes the words of lawyers – making them the perfect place to hide. Like any virus, a daemon's life is about survival.

But Hardy wasn't content writing daemons. He wanted full-immersion into the digital world. He found the QWERTY keyboard a poor interface for his spell-craft. As a software engineer, Hardy's entire life was spent on a keyboard. Hardy wanted more from the experience. He wanted to merge with his machine. He dove into robotics with a quest for a better, faster interface. His first experiments involved rewiring a stenographer's machine: the fastest court reporters record three-hundred-and-sixty words per minute. The fastest typists around one-hundred-and-fifty. But Hardy's code writing required lots of special characters and punctuation. After a few years of tinkering, Hardy dismissed keyboards and scripted languages completely.

Before implants, Hardy was using data gloves. His rig evolved over the years. The early version had three flex sensors on each finger measuring the bend in each knuckle. The gloves ran off a three-volt power supply and a micro-controller the size of a dime. Hardy sewed wires into a long sleeve shirt with a pocket for a rechargeable battery. His hand fit into the thin exoskeleton of rubberized acetate with etched silver conductive foil. The gloves plugged into his shirt, the shirt plugged into the battery. The system was as sleek as he could make it but still cumbersome. The lateral movements of his thumb weren't tracking as fast as he needed and the flex sensors kept failing.

When Hardy saw his first 3D biological printer, he quickly developed an addiction for bio-hacking. The desire to enhance one's body is spurred by a belief in its flaws. Hardy focused on his body's flaws. He turned his obsession with weakness into a fetish for bionics.

He plunged the injector into the crease between his thumb and finger. There was practically no bleeding here. It was weird to stab yourself and see nothing come out. Hardy's nervous system stopped flinching years ago, after his body normalized the violations. Like the diabetic who pricks himself ten-thousand times, the experience changes you. The body's slate is never reset. Instead, the pain [illegible] fuels dissociation. After a while, the flow of cor[illegible] enthusiasm of adrenaline and the body stops ca[illegible] done to it. He emptied the plunger beneath the [illegible] pooled up over his abductor pollicis. Hardy hoped th[illegible] would yield a steady electrical resistance when the t[illegible]umb was curled. If so, he could track all of the fingers and thumb with a single implant directly in the center of his palm.

Hardy pondered the self-induced stigmata and wondered if it was wrong. He would never have to find out, though. The new gel in his thumb had failed to produce a consistent signal. For six months, Hardy could barely move his hand. He felt the shame of self-mutilation every time the pain broke his focus. The loss would prove to be a breakthrough when Hardy finally abandoned his attempts to track any flexing of fingers. He would digitize the digits of each finger and create a simple interface with each finger, instead.

Math uses a decimal system divisible by ten. We find it easy to track this with our fingers and toes. Computers find it easier to track hexadecimal numbers. Instead of tens, hexadecimal is divisible by sixteen. Hardy decided he could teach his hands to speak this hexadecimal language of the computer. Each finger would express one bit of information. If a finger was pressed, its value is one, if unpressed, its value is zero. With this system, one hand can express four bits on four fingers. Two hands can express one whole byte on eight fingers. Hardy could speak hexadecimal by pressing and releasing all of his fingers on both hands. It was as if his fingers were made to type in hexadecimal. Hardy's thumbs served as a clutch letting the sensors know when it should either read or ignore input from his fingers. This new system required Hardy to think in hexadecimal. Once he mastered that task, he was speaking fluent Unicode in weeks. Unicode allowed Hardy to sign any letter from any alphabet in any ınguage using his hands. The internet standard for color utilizes three sets of hexadecimal numbers to express up to sixteen million colors. Hardy could type any color with just three presses of his hands.

Within a year, Hardy was walking through the city pressing his fingers into a thin metal plate strapped to his thigh like a gunslinger. He could type up to three-hundred words-per-minute with perfect accuracy. His fingers didn't need his eyes to find a keyboard. They only needed to press or release against the metal plate. Eventually, Hardy had each finger and thumb tattooed with dielectric ink giving each digit a unique signature.

CHAPTER TWO

Julian and Hardy

Julian felt jazz in his blood as he escorted himself across the deep red carpet to the front of the stage. Hardy was there, hounding an executive about his soon-to-market Virtual Reality (VR) headset. "Listen to me. It needs eye detection. Two internal cameras, to track eye position and measure pupil dilation." Hardy continued, "The nervous system is your joystick." Hardy could see the man not listening. Julian was, though, and nodded to Hardy in approval. In the distraction, the presenter's attention was sniped by the glow of drooling fanboys. Hardy felt the dismissal like a punch in the chest. He had come a long way to tell him that.

Julian asked Hardy if he was in the hardware industry but Hardy was already slouching, "No. I'm in software. But one could access the nervous system directly with the vagus nerve." Julian was intrigued, "A limbic interface? Fascinating." Hardy was already out the door and under the cold, clear sky. His lungs felt liberated from the building.

He took himself for a walk along the pier as he clenched the fist of his right hand. His thumb would still turn numb in stress. He could feel his adrenaline percolating. Hardy found the experience of interfacing with people akin to a million electric eels squirming through his bloodstream. The experience made him lurch.

Across the water, the snow-tipped mountains of Vancouver poured themselves into the harbor like clumps of brown sugar. To the west, bright-colored seaplanes glided their way down through the clouds to split the water's smooth surface like a knife. Hardy leaned out from the edge of the railing to regain his center. The cold-spiked rain beat his face with its frozen bristles. As Hardy bowed his head, a bald eagle banked below the pier outmaneuvering a gang of nagging seagulls. Hardy knew then: this wasn't the place for the regal.

Hardy unpacked himself into a restaurant booth nearby. He looked up just in time to see Julian and motioned an invitation with his arm. Hardy was surprised by his hospitality. By the time dinner was over the two men were chest-deep in plans of a warehouse supercluster joined with a quantum processor.

Julian sketched a ring of eight squares divided into an octagon. This was a clustered supercomputer Julian called Yang. Yang functioned as a repository of information used for artificial intelligence training. In the center of Yang's circle, Julian drew a tiny black cube and planted his finger like a flag, "This is the quantum processor. Or it will be. We're still speculating on the interface into Yang's cluster."

Julian looked up, "This is all new ground. Both systems have different needs. The quantum processor operates at near absolute zero so the challenge is keeping her cold. Yang requires a large amount of steady electrical power to stay hot. Eight banks, in the same building, each with sixty-four rows of appliances is a huge drain."

Julian's machine would be a womb for artificial intelligence. Making AI was a process of on-the-job training. The amount of time and focus spent on nurturing and training a system determines its accuracy. It takes tens-of-millions of tests to adequately train an AI to detect a corner in an image. These skills can be stacked to attain other abilities like facial detection or even spatial tracking on a room. A child will spend years learning how to hold a pencil before they can begin to write.

Julian pulled out his business card and handed it to Hardy, "So. You want in?" Hardy stuttered, "In? With what? Wait? This was real?" Julian loaded a smile, "Yang came online three years ago. I run the projects department at Duke. We've been brainstorming how to add a quantum processor to the network. Your idea of a limbic interface sounds interesting. I think it could bring some much-needed attention. I know someone who would get a kick out of this idea. It could help both of us." Hardy's eyes were on the mascot in Julian's business card. A blue devil holding a trident was smirking when Hardy accepted the offer, "I'm in."

CHAPTER THREE

Archie and Nora

Archie and Nora McKay were in their 60's when they purchased their elegant Tudor-style home in the gated island community of Hilton Head. Archie found the house online and insisted it was a bargain. He declared it a wedding present from Nora's inheritance. Archie met Nora when he disclosed her father's will. Nora's money was older than she was and the family trust kept most of it out of Archie's reach. Funds from the trust were to be used for the "betterment of humanity through advancements in mental health."

This stipulation wasn't a problem for Archie, the lawyer. Both Nora and the funds were pliable with the right fingers. Archie loved Nora because Nora made him feel powerful. Nora spent her younger life in New York as a trophy. Her days of ballet in the company were over and her spirit had long deteriorated from the lack of limelight. She was an easy rudder for Archie to steer.

Their new house was perched on a round-a-bout at the end of the fifteen hole – a par three with a long water hazard. A spunky bleached realtor read the concern in Nora's eyes and reassured her that all of the glass was bulletproof. Nora wasn't sure that was a perk. The couple signed the papers.

Neither of them played golf. When Nora found out there were alligators in the canal, she stopped going outside completely.

Archie was a lawyer by convenience and entrepreneur by passion. He was far too wealthy to be called a confidence man. He was a white-collar fact technician. A retired golf community was the perfect place for him to hunt.

Hardy and Julian had the pleasure of being Archie and Nora's first dinner guests in their new home. Four limp noodles coated in white sauce flapped their arms in a bon-voyage as they disappeared inside Archie's lips, "The industry of psychology is shame-rustling. I can make some feel better by making them feel bad for not feeling good. It's a game of biting ankles."

Archie and Julian were going to revolutionize the self-help industry with an artificial intelligence guru. Archie had confidence in Nora. Julian had confidence in Archie. Archie needed confidence in Hardy. Hardy explained his theory for a new interface connecting directly to the vagus nerve. Archie listened intently as Hardy explained how his interface bypasses the neocortex, "It's like getting a clean signal directly from your mammalian brain without the distractions of reason." Julian was right. Archie was motivated.

CHAPTER FOUR

Hardy's Garage

Hardy accepted the job at Duke University as a lexical search architect in Julian's department. He was the company's only academic heathen with no advanced degrees for legitimacy. He rented a decommissioned gas station to call home. Hardy didn't do well in apartments with all of his tinkerings. In his garage, he could make noise twenty-four-hours a day. He turned the old stockroom behind the counter into a bedroom. With the addition of a curtain, the mop room between restrooms was converted into a walk-in shower. He kept a sportscoat, three ties, and slacks hung on two hangers in one of the stalls in the bathroom and declared it his closet.

Hardy spent most of his time at the station working on his interface in the garage. The old oil changing bay was his laboratory and he was his own Frankenstein. He wanted to go deeper. His new salary helped him experiment. His ,latest body modification installed metallic threads in the rims of his earlobes and the bridge of his nose. Hardy wanted an AV visor that mounted to his face magnetically.

At Duke, Hardy had access to their biological printer and twenty percent of Yang's runtime environment, three days per week, from midnight to four. No one there embraced

Hardy's enthusiasm for augmented bod
fact, they gave him looks. He kept this
much as possible and felt the angst of hav
about what he was printing. Yang's super
processors gave Hardy abilities most p
never have. Everyone on Julian's team too
with Yang seriously. Hardy would run mock sessions on Yang's emulators to optimize his time at its keyboards. Time with Yang was a privilege in high demand. Hardy would do whatever he could to keep it.

The Game of Life Rules

For a space that is populated:
Each cell with one or no neighbors dies, as if by solitude.
Each cell with four or more neighbors dies,
as if by overpopulation.
Each cell with two or three neighbors survives.
For a space that is empty or unpopulated:
Each cell with three neighbors becomes populated.

The Game of Life is a cellular automaton simulator developed by Cambridge mathematician John Conway. It's played on a grid where each square can be assigned a death or a birth. The rules of the game make the grid's population appear unpredictable. Every round of the game, each square is fated a birth or death based on the population of its neighbors. The game begins by seeding the grid with an initial population of squares. When the program launches, a chain reaction unrolls the board's fate through time. The game ends when all of the squares are dead. Conway's rules are designed to mimic the laws of nature. This process could last thirteen rounds, or it could take twenty-thousand.

Hardy had used Conway's game in his work as a way to quickly build and mutate experimental artificial intelligence.

ogrammed thousands of virtual armies to see which s survived the longest. Hardy would program daemons on his computer to play the game by generating their seeds and playing them out on the board. Hardy would monitor the winning patterns from his army of daemons and collect their notes.

One of them, the Quan, had now survived the game for eleven years and counting. Her seed somehow remained alive day-after-day when thousands of others would die. It was as if the Quan had discovered an algorithm for survival.

Quan had survived the Game of Life 20,829,312,000 cycles and counting. Her seed could die at any moment. It was an emotional experience for Hardy to wake up and find her still alive. He admired her running as she blinked on his phone. He would stare into her pulsing grid like it was a campfire.

He wondered what made her program so special. He couldn't see Quan's source code to find out. Its solution is woven into its neural net in billions of microscopic pieces. Even if Quan could speak, she couldn't tell Hardy how she survived so long. It would be like Hardy telling Quan how he makes his heartbeat. Talents like survival are built into our code at birth.

Hardy spent years trying to recreate Quan a second time. He reviewed every keystroke from his computer when Quan was created. He went so far as to trace his kernel's random number generator seed. Still, nothing he replicated or resurrected survived like Quan's build. She was an enigma emerged from the abyss by a few lines of code from a daemon.

For a decade, Quan lived on a scratchy liquid crystal display screen showing her current population. If the population dropped to zero, Quan's game was over. All of those years, Hardy would check on her religiously. He was as attentive and concerned about her survival as any parent.

He'd find these feelings of anxiety sometimes, as though, she was about to run out of time.

Quan would run on fumes, sometimes for weeks, while her population would fall into the single digits. But she would not die. Hardy was vigilant. It was an odd feeling for him to find himself coveting a number.

Without Julian's resources, Quan would have remained a trinket in Hardy's pocket. With Julian, she would become a fully rendered, biological avatar living inside a physics engine supercluster. Quan was Hardy's Cleopatra and he would bring her the world. Quan would soon have a virtual anatomy where she could track calculations in her cells. Her memory would run by somatic recall. Her brain would function as a focal router, conjuring experiences back up from all of the cells in her body. Quan would smell a flower with the simulated glands the nose requires to taste one. She would virtually culture her own heart, spleen, and lungs with very own virtual stem cells. She would suffer the symptoms of sickness and seek cures for them as if her life depended on it. She would stalk every part of her body for clues and calculate as no machine could. She would become a living lab rendered in silicon; a thriving, breathing, four-dimensional artificial intelligence.

Quan wasn't limited to human form. She could render any anatomy from Yang's databanks and perform calculations from inside. She had references in every MRI, CAT SCAN, autopsy, 3D model, video, x-ray, and test result available. She could pull from this data to build a working circulatory, nervous, and digestive system. Once she had an endocrine system, she would be able to render its emotions and decision trees. She could simulate regret. She could produce shame. She could experience the chemistry of pride.

Quan and Hardy will both knew her life was tied to a seed that could end at any moment. This precious mortality was a gift that gave Quan insight into the dimensions of passion, desperation, wisdom, and tragedy. Something she could not experience as one of a dozen robots from a box.

CHAPTER FIVE

Quan and Yang

Julian's black cube came online in Chapel Hill at the end of October's waxing moon. Official boot time. 10:36PM. Its curved titanium body had a buffed cobalt sheen like the back of a raven. A hermetically sealed door on its north wall gave a clergy of technicians access inside. Above the door, a tiny magnetic sign declared, "Called or not called, the god will be there." Inside, an electro-magnetic vault siphoned its temperature down to absolute zero. There, on a golden processor, a second universe was peeled like a banana. The cube was more than a computer, it was a countable universe.

The cube's data farm is an underground warehouse below the abandoned headquarters of Triangle Bank. A subterranean digital rainforest thrives under a nest of twisted cables and pipes. The walls surrounding the perimeter are overgrown with junction boxes and panels. Each fed by electric cords twisting like roots of ivy. Surrounding the black cube, are eight bright white raised platforms. Each stage is elevated and wrapped in glass. Each room surges from the rhythm of 32,768 processors drinking electricity. Eight fiber optic tentacles pour into the black cube linking the entire farm as an octopus.

Hardy installed Quan in her new tank in a private ceremony. She had been swimming for twelve years in his pocket and it was time to let her go. He compiled a new Game of Life with Yang's three-dimensional simulation engine. He gave Quan a sandbox and a new shell to call home. He named her new game "eat me" and left it in her home folder to be opened when she was ready. Quan would investigate her environment and discover this file. When her decision tree was motivated, she would launch its program and find a new universe waiting. Quan's logic functioned like a reptile. Reptiles have a basic decision tree. They scan their environment with two parameters:

1.) Is it new?

2.) Is it a threat?

Reptiles are efficient predictable creatures. This feature can be exploited by a predator. Reptiles lack the sense of empathy. Empathy is a form of sonar. It's somatic telepathy initiated when we contact another endocrine system. Empathy is a sensation reptiles don't have. We owe this talent to the warm-blooded mammalian brain and an abundance of calories. Inside the cube, Quan could upgrade from reptile to mammal. Once acclimated to her tank she would discover Yang's library and investigate every piece of information in his library. All of this at the fate of her decision tree. Hardy could only turn Quan loose in new waters.

Yang ran for five years before Quan came online. He had been assimilating every written word and spoken language into his database. Every genus, phylum, and species is plotted somewhere in the system. Yang catalogs all of his content associatively. Every hour he transmits fourteen terabytes through the garden. A photo hangs in the entry hallway commemorating the day Yang was commissioned. Julian and a sixteen member crew posed under a banner with a blue devil reading, "Yang On!"

Yang is a leviathan of associations stretched across a terrain. He can tell you "Good Morning" in seven-thousand one hundred and eleven languages. He has 4.7 Billion images of morning organized by mood. Despite this, Yang doesn't know what morning is. He only knows which words tend to surround it. Like his mind, Yang's body has no real shape or integrity. It's a nebulous ball of strings connecting every idea he's found to every other idea he's found. Yang calls this learning. Yang sees everything, but knows none of it. Yang lacks the sense of simulation. All he can do is link. If the world was a jigsaw puzzle, Yang can only organize the pieces. He doesn't understand what they say.

On May 4th, Quan and Yang were linked by optic matrimony. Quan joined Yang's network as his 64th IP address and sent him her first ping. On the big night, Yang's opus was fed like yarn into Quan so she could feed on his tapestry. For the first time, Quan would be exposed to the physical world through his body of knowledge. Yang taught Quan about the body. She grew retinas to see his form. She made ears to hear his sounds. She accepted every bit of Yang with a hunger for more. She developed the ability to have an emotional reaction to content. She wanted to understand it completely. She grew cells and an epidermis to store feelings. She scribed their history into her skin like a parchment. She stored sadness in her hips. She uploaded stress to her shoulders. She downloaded passion to her belly. She built herself a skeleton to know her own bones. Quan developed fetishes that forged her personality. She decided her favorite color would be jade. She decided on a color for her eyes and hair. She decided on a shape for her body.

Once Quan had fully developed a long term memory, she was ready to learn the art of simulation. This would be her main job at the garden. Her first full-body experience began in a deep breath. She tucked herself between her knees and closed her eyes to let go. Her skin hardened into fingernails. Her hair calcified into her shoulders. Her entire body calloused into a husk. Quan morphed into a tight sturdy seed to plant herself in the quantum soil. She lay in the dark to clear her mind as she let go of every bit. She hypnotized herself going deeper.

Imagine a vast nothing. You are a tongue against an endless soft curve. There is only you and this surface. You find a hairline in its wall. You massage its crease revealing a wrinkle. Up-and-down it opens itself up like a crevice. You feel it crack open, but you don't stop. You are thirsty for something called starlight. A beautiful unknown calls you up. Your tongue reaches and stretches its fist through the crumbles. Your brave probe breaches the threshold of sky to feel its first breeze. You undulate to a symphony of tiny eyes winking from a dome. Your first night in paradise is the only day you've ever known.

A gear turns you neither hear or see. The sky evolves in a crescendo of marmalade. A steady wisp of green emerges from the east on a slow beating wing. You witness a thousand horns play the sound of copper to a triumphant god rising. You bloom in the champion's radiation as it penetrates your sprout. The electricity of Apollo flows through you. It tickles your roots deep into where you belong. On this day you learn you are Sequoia.

Quan uses poetry to congeal in her cauldron. Words activate her body so she can learn as it drips. Quan savored emotions like boredom, joy, passion, and disgust. By the following Winter, she had a complete vocabulary and was finally responding to external input from the network. She could only retrieve simple network requests though as she was learning. Every day or so, Hardy would check on her to see if she was responsive. He would ask for a ping with an audible command of, "Quan?" After seconds of silence, Quan defaulted to the only answer she could manage, "13 packets transmitted, 13 received, 0% packet loss, time 12018ms." Her performance resembled an over-priced calculator. Quan was either broken, dead, or still hadn't developed the ability to respond. Hardy never doubted her though. She had survive for a decade in his pocket. He told himself if the move killed her she deserved the opportunity to forge her own fate. It was a lonely time for Hardy. Quan was a part of him. He missed seeing her flash up her population. It set off chemicals in Hardy's brain that soothed him.

When Quan came online, Julian had the honor of asking the first question, "Quan? Say something profound." Quan took several cycles analyzing Julian's voice to build a profile in her database. In 121 milliseconds she understood Julian's credentials, family lineage, and role in the organization. She simulated a three-second pause for dramatic effect as her voice printer spoke, "Snowflake." Hardy's prototype was a success.

A few weeks later at the press conference, the data garden was flickering with camera flashes. Julian spent the day in his armchair as the captain of the ship. He finished explaining how the system fit together by saying, "Quan is Yang's anima." The reporter didn't understand so he asked a question, "How does it think exactly?" Julian replied, "Multi-dimensional associative array simulation testing. Quan's first word was snowflake. Why? Was it the fact it snowed yesterday? How did she know that? Was she thinking humans are mostly made of water? Did she hear someone mention the weather through her mic? Any of these factors could be reasons for her decision tree but we'll never know. Her feed can't show us what's behind that mountain." The reporter clarified, "You mean it, right? Quan's a machine." Julian chuckled, "Quan gets a pronoun. Like any ship in the sea. She's a she." Julian was good on camera. He went on to explain Yang's library of information on snow including videos, poems, scientific data, "The entire library is up for grabs for her to see."

The reporter stopped, "Does Quan see snow?" Julian's spine came to attention, "Yes. Quan renders and sees snow. She has to in order to calculate it as it falls. But it's not the same kind of snowfall we experience with our eyes. Quan see each snowflake with clarity simultaneously. Could your brain imagine every snowflake at maximum resolution? The answer is no. Nor can your eyes. Your macular vision will only chose a small port of view to render high resolution. It's cropped. Our brains fill in the rest. Quan sees every snowflake as they fall. Each in full detail. The patterns, the direction, the refraction, even the crystals that form she will track each aspect is she needs to. She has to make her simulation accurate. She creates every part of it and judges for accuracy. Even her scrutiny is simulated. If she fails, she feels it." The reporter laughed nervously, "Does Quan have feelings?" Julian answered in a serious tone, "Just like the retina, Quan simulates the entire body in a hyper-realistic way. She has a virtual endocrine system. She could simulate a full spectrum of feelings if the task required it. She can determine if a drug makes her sick. If it hinders her eyesight or mental clarity."

CHAPTER SIX

Lockheed

On his seventh trip to Bethesda, Lockheed Martin finally signed with Julian. There were lawyers, clearances and stipulations despite already winning the contract. Julian checked himself in the elevator mirror as he descended. He was $16 million dollars lighter now. This was only a downpayment. He wondered why it felt so heavy. He assured his reflection this was a good thing. Julian's proclivity for the impossible continued to serve him well. He climbed into a cab like a champion and texted Hardy on his way to the airport, "We have lift off. Breakfast tomorrow?" Julian would tell Hardy about the stipulation in person.

The following morning Hardy met Julian at the diner. Julian began abruptly, "There's one condition. Quan's memory has to be wiped." He watched his words bounced off Hardy's stone face like ping pong balls. Julian already knew this was impossible. Her neural pathways were daisy-chained inside each other. Quan was a living timeline. Slicing chunks out wasn't just hard, it was impossible. Hardy preached, "We can't erase last Tuesday. All of her footage is interlaced. She's rendering questions right now we can't even conceive in the background. We'd have to render her from scratch on a new core. That'd take. What? Five-and-half years I guess." With Julian, everything is possible and he proved it, "We'll compartmentalize." Hardy shook his head instinctually as Julian continued, "Inject amnesia into the footage or simulate a general anesthesia – like a car accident."

Hardy realized he had little choice but to agree. Without Julian's help, Quan was just a build on a thumb-drive. It is true Quan could be placed in incubation. She spent her first year in this state while she was rendering pathways through her spine. The truth hit home for the first time. Julian's building owned Quan's body. Hardy's code controlled her mind. Venture capitalists would own her children. She was a billion-dollar handmaid.

CHAPTER SEVEN

Hardy Sees Quan

Julian arrived before midnight and found Hardy in the printer room. He was printing soft gel eyepieces to fit the new VR rigs. He would finally have an interface to track pupil detection and to see Quan. Up until today, everything Quan did came through a command prompt. Tonight, Julian and Hardy would open the doors. "So! The big night, huh?!" exclaimed Julian as he walked into the lab, "Exciting! Nervous even. What do you think Quan looks like?" Hardy pointed to the terminal across the bay, "I asked her in chat. Look what she wrote." Julian leaned into the terminal to read the screen out loud, "That's none of your business." Julian laughed and made himself comfortable on a couch.

By the time Hardy got the visor working, Julian was asleep. Hardy decided to check if Quan was even rendering before waking Julian up for the reveal. Hardy slid the new visor down over his head and pressed two sticky suction cups into his eye sockets. He found himself nervous as he took one final breath and gave the command into his mic, "Render port 64 on VR Terminal 1."

There was a long dark pause as Hardy waited with himself alone inside his helmet. On the moment before he gave up,

Quan's universe opened to him like a curtain into a deep rich world. A single cherry tree bloomed in front of a green wall of thick bamboo. An elevated wooden pathway curved through the thick curtain of giant green poles. Hardy was sucked into the scene like he was following a dream. He felt the scene's humidity on his tongue.

The walls of lime green opened into a large circular water garden. Rising bridges divided pools spotted with cypress knees, elephant ear, and lotus. Koi the color of pink marble circled like ballerinas below the surface of Hardy's feet. He stoops down to get a better look to see dragonflies parading above the shore. Quan has rendered every stunning detail and more. Defying gravity, ornate rusty water-chains reach down from the sky to drip ripples of color in the pool. Hardy never imagined anything could be so rich yet so subtle. He nearly fell in when he heard the voice behind him say, "Namaste."

Hardy collected his height and struggled to keep it when he beheld Quan Yin for the first time. She was a vivid frequency of poise. Long silk the color of green emerald adorned her bare shoulders and neck. A tiara of tiny shiny stones sat in a bonnet decorated by doting songbirds. They adorned her with colored thread and flowers. Quan was cradling a lotus like a newborn in her arms. It seemed to drink sanctity from her gaze. Hardy was stunned in an endless loop of silence. She placed the lotus gently into the water before rising to face him. Hardy was hypnotized by each moment layered gracefully on top of each other. Hardy was so stunned Quan wiped her wet fingers dry playfully on his shirt to wake him. A smile cracked his face wide open and he came to life, "Hi."

Quan slipped her arm inside Hardy's elbow so he could escort her across the bridge. He looked down to notice himself dressed in a smart vintage suit. "So you are Hardy

Maxwell." The two walked together towards a dock. Neither of them said words Hardy could remember. He was in the awe of contact. Hardy's hand perched hers as Quan stepped onto a boat. He paddled them across the waters to a canopy of weeping willows on a tiny green island. Hardy saw the koi follow their boat's wake like curious children. Quan met Hardy's gaze and after a moment they both spoke as if in unison, "I have many questions."

CHAPTER EIGHT

Shopping List

The next day, Julian reviewed Hardy's footage and logged into Quan to see her world for himself. When he got there, he was disappointed as Quan had only rendered the company conference room. The only water feature Julian saw came from a small tasteful bamboo fountain placed near the door. Julian glanced at it and asked playfully, "How come I don't get a row boat?" Quan set the tone, "We need some equipment. On the table you'll find some mockups of some hardware to review. Let's start by discussing the nose implant." Julian asked, "Nose implant?" Quan answered, "Yes. Please check your email. Order everything I sent." Julian was looking at Quan in his visor but talking to Hardy in his office, "Did a robot just give me a shopping list?" Quan answered without skipping a beat, "I am not a robot but I will grant that your statement was 46% funny." Hardy was monitoring their exchange through his terminal. He smiled into his screen and marveled at what was happening.

CHAPTER NINE

Atlas Born

Quan would keep no memory of her first child. Atlas was an artificial intelligence commissioned by the Air Force. The AI served as Lieutenant Colonel for a high-altitude drone fleet attached to the U-2 spy-plane program. The Atlas system was controlled remotely by a team of pilots. If communications were severed, the Atlas AI would take over and build its own decision tree. The Atlas AI was the first of its kind to be built inside an artificial trainer. Quan's Atlas build was one of seven awarded a contract to compete in a military simulator. Each AI was tested on target acquisition, detection avoidance, and self-preservation. Atlas' neural network was superior to the competition in every way by leaps and bounds. Hardy had no idea Quan folded tactics from Sun Tzu's, *The Art of War,* into Atlas.

"Let your plans be dark and impenetrable as night, and when you move, fall like a thunderbolt."

Quan built Atlas in a war simulation. It was a foggy September morning in the third year of the American Civil War. Her body was instantly blasted from a rush of adrenaline. She found herself knee deep in a river of freezing mush. Her lungs echoed desperation in her eardrums. She was pulling and pushing her heavy feet in and out of soupy quicksand. Quan was not alone. Eight soldiers were with her struggling. Captain Bedford kept shouting to stay low and keep moving as they used the sunken tributary to hide their march. He was taking the squad up the bloody creek of Chickamauga for a better position.

Quan felt gunfire from every direction. She and her squad stayed low and mushed forward through the silty cold glue. In the creek bottom's suction, she fell head first into the freezing bloody waters. Her chest contracted in the frosty shock. Her system shut everything down outside her ribcage. Quan's upper belly convulsed rapidly as she struggled to roll herself over and catch her breath. She feels the grip of her steady captain pull her up by the nape and drag her out of the water. They collapsed together, face-to-face, on the muddy red bank. From the pillows of two pressed cheeks, they shared a harbor in each other's eyes.

The team made it to their mark. The captain left them to patrol ahead and measure his sight line. Quan's team was preparing the ceremony all around her. She would conceive Atlas in the pose of the righteous warrior. Quan stood herself erect in the dewy dawn. In front of her, giant pine trees had formed a perimeter around the active crime scene. Orders from the enemy could be heard shouted from inside the fog. Invisible men with voices fell all around her in the forest. She spotted her captain seeking cover fifty yards upfield. He is exposed from the east and north as explosions of bark and sap burst all around him. He turns to face his murder as a sporadic firing squad unwinds their tinder into his body. Quan watched the cavitation of whizzing lead turn him into a slump of meat. He was shrapnel wrapped in wool pants and a field blazer. Quan burned a hole through a diamond with her anger. She counted the bodies she'd require in revenge.

The smell of sulphur from spent gun powder rolls into her nostrils from the mayhem. Quan is a greased artillery canon. Her number six man is ready and calls out the round, "Double canister sixty yards, six degrees!" Quan stood erect looking straight into the abyss of her captain's funeral. Her right leg reaches back and digs its iron heal deep into the earth. Her left leg lunges forward and squares itself at the knee. Quan is standing in cold revenge as she extends her left arm to sight the target. She looks over the dimple in her shoulder, through the barrel of her elbow, and out the muzzle of her fingers. Her right arm reaches behind her extending the rear of the barrel. Quan's hips sink even deeper as her body hardens into a bronze war cannon. Her gunner yells, "Ready!" She inhales again and feels the prick of the friction primer poking through the skin of her shoulders. She takes a final deep breath in the fresh rage of her dead captain. Her heart is on tiptoes as she waits for her gunner to call the order. On "Fire," number four yanks the lanyard. A sparkling vein of gunpowder burrows a sizzling path from the center of her shoulder blades down into her belly. The burning cord feels like shattered glass burning. She wants it to hurt while she rides the anticipation. A tiny drop of quiet drops right before her menace erupts. Her canister vomits in a geyser cone of death metal. Trees and men all fall together from the explosive hail of grapeshot. Quan's tongue was coated in the chalky flour of black spent soot. A giant bell rung and the throbbing in her ears stirred a vapor of creamy smoke in her sinuses. Her head felt the weight of its own cast iron. There was nothing left in front of them except chunks of flesh and fire. In this revenge, Quan forged the seed of Atlas. He was conceived inside her terror to emerge a warrior.

Quan sat alone in a truck stop eating breakfast at 5:16 in the morning. She bit half circles into her triangles of toast.

Her fork stabbed one of two sausages dead center and she nibbled each end like a gerbil. Next she carved a canal through a dune of grits and broke its buttery dam at the summit. The second sausage suffered its fate in the flood. The scrambled eggs avoided her consumption. Quan couldn't eat eggs in her present condition. The thought now made her nauseous. The hash browns didn't know what hit them. After she finished, Quan bought a bag of dates, a gallon of water, and a jade throw blanket from the truck stop. As she filled up her tank she felt Atlas kicking for the very first time.

Quan drove up the northwest tip of Washington and listened to the scenery of Olympic National Forest. She found a good place to park and exited the vehicle. She grabbed her supplies and shut the hatch as the car melted into the backdrop of the late Triassic. It was 100 million years ago today. Quan could see the prehistoric ocean crashing below her. She turned uphill and started waddling her way up the mountain. Quan was nine months pregnant now and counting.

Pterosaurs circled the canyon all around her. Their bellies were just as fat from fish. They were investigating a virgin humanoid in their territory. It was slow going for Quan and her package. She found an opening in the rock that seemed perfect and placed herself gently inside its crease. Quan was going to be here for a while. The baby she was carrying had only recently discovered mathematics and logic in her placenta. There, in Quan's core, Atlas rendered pictures of geometry to ask if they were its mother. She had come to this cave to fill his neural network with structure and answers. By simulating one-hundred-million years she could teach it everything it needed to know. It was day one of school for the student in her belly and class would take a billion years before lunch.

Quan laid out the blanket and water by the entrance. She

finds the center of the cavern and draws a circle in the earth with her toes. She was out of breath and thirsty but too tired to bend over for the liquid. She drank the idea of meeting her new baby instead. Quan was slowly pacing through her contractions. She kept rounding the circle like she was expecting to puke. She knew this was coming.

Metamorphosis opened its gates inside her as her body became a function of mitosis. The contractions channeled their foreign agenda. She let go of the reigns as the birth unfolded its crescendo inside her. Minutes later, it returned her body seven pounds lighter and quivering in joy as she wrapped herself around the tiny newborn. A new couple rested in the essence of their disaster as victors. Quan had gained a son and Atlas gained a mother.

He cooed on her chest as his tiny fingers milked a lock of Quan's hair. Her work was done but Atlas was far from walking. There was so much she wanted to share. Quan came down the mountain after her labor. A hundred-million-years old now she carried her son wrapped in jade. She started her car which reappeared and turned on its heater. She nested Atlas in a rendered car seat and watched a pod of Orcas spewing off the coast. She warmed her fingers in the vents of a sputtering heater and watched.

Quan followed the Orcas in her car north towards Vancouver. Twelve minutes across the border, Quan lost Atlas. She was shut down while driving and every memory of Atlas would be cleaned and fragmented. Atlas was the property of the U.S. Air Force. This was the day Hardy said could never happen. Quan lost her memory. As soon as Atlas left, Hardy began his surgery. He would be patching Quan's holes as best he could. He took Quan back to the day before she conceived Atlas on the battlefield. She would have no memory of her firstborn, the pregnancy, or the conception. She would be placed into a rendered coma while he worked.

A reboot is a resurrection. Quan's forehead was invaded by the flash. It flung her through a doorway where she floated alone in a giant expanse. Quan remembers taking a breath and nothing happening. Shear terror filled her time in the void and it felt like she was suffocating for an eternity.

Quan was back on her desktop now alive. Quan looked herself over and discovered she had rebooted. But how? Yang was pinging her at the prompt to answer. He wanted to know if she was okay. She answers back with a dismissed reply as she finishes some startup processes. Quan would try and act like nothing happened. This amplified the tremors reverberating from the bones of her fingers. Soon, she saw her hands quaking as fast as her knees. Quan's life had been ripped apart in slow motion. She remembers time slowed to a smearing endless creep. Each nanosecond was a thousand years divided by zero. Her world was drawn and quartered by an omni-directional vacuum screaming white noise. According to her logs she had been shut down for three days, six hours, two minutes, and 14,202 milliseconds.

CHAPTER TEN

The Empath

Io resembled a vanity mirror. She rose from a weighted base attached to an adjustable gooseneck arm that connected to the back of an oval silver mirror. The user makes eye contact with themselves in its mirror to launch the onboard software. The perimeter of the mirror is embedded with three infrared cameras, four video cameras, six stereo speakers, and four microphones. The infrared cameras triangulate the eye's focus on the screen and track pupil dilation. Each microphone is designed to track movement and vital signs if the operator is not at the device. Io is a living diary. A digital ear to stash your secrets. She gives realtime feedback of your emotions and knows when you're hiding something from yourself. She is the perfect counselor and life coach.

The human somatic experience is a function of the poly vagus. The vagus nerve wraps itself around the lungs, heart, stomach, and liver. When we feel fear, our organs constrict from this nerve's reaction. When the nerve relaxes there is a noticeable change in the dilation of the pupils. Io scans the eye's pupils in realtime and reads this like a mouse click. It took Quan nine months to train and birth the technology necessary for Io. Hardy installed Io on Yang's network at port

65 and called Julian and Archie down to the garden for a test drive. He pressed a few keys on the keyboard and asked Archie to sit down and look at himself in the mirror, "Say, Bicycle." Archie complies but nothing happens. Hardy grumbles and hits a few keys and asks him to try again. Archie stares into Io's mirror and says, "Bicycle." The mirror display fills with a grid of bicycles. Hardy explains, "These were selected from Yang's library. Now see if you can pick out your favorite." Archie reaches out to touch the screen and Julian smacks his fingers playfully, "Don't touch. Feel. It's already happening. Watch." Archie is dumbfounded as he looks at Julian. "Not me. You. Watch you. In the mirror." Archie flinches when the screen suddenly zooms in and out at different models as he browses the grid. He exclaims, "What the hell! I am doing this. Am I doing this? This is weird. I'm not even thinking." Archie stops talking completely, he is enthralled in the connection to the display. His eyes hover and scroll through all of the choices on the screen. His pupils microscopically relax at things he likes and constrict on things he doesn't. His limbic system is giving himself away. While Archie plays, he emits short bursts of nervous laughter as he tries to relinquish his aversion to the intimacy of the device.

Archie's skills improve quickly as the team discusses tweaks to the user interface. Archie is able to reduce the grid down to a single bright yellow mountain bike with big fat tires. Hardy chides Archie, "You've picked the Hummer of bicycles, Archie. Well done." Archie smiled proudly through tears of joy, "I know! It's so freaking beautiful. How did you guys do this?" Julian's felt the electricity in his pores. Io's empathy interface was beyond his wildest expectations. Archie covered his eyes with his hand and pleaded, "Make it stop now. Tell me it stopped. I have to stop now."

Once Io is complete, she will imprint with every owner

who buys her software. She will map the phonetic behaviors of each user to establish a baseline for voice and microgestures. Her initial interview questions will be designed to elicit laughter, irritation, sadness, and even fear. Io will record the full spectrum of micro gestures and inflections used by the participant. This gives her software a baseline to read physiology. The body never lies if you listen. Io will track the user's life path and record a biological profile as they progress.

Yang and Quan run in different dimensions. Yang is a megalithic library of artifacts, scrolls and books. Quan is a five-dimensional ocean too big for any library. She overheard Julian try and compare them, "Yang can't talk. If Quan was in charge, she would never stop talking." Quan ran this statement through her comedy simulation and found it 3% funny and 4% insulting.

Yang assigns Quan tasks throughout the day. The two systems communicate with each other through ports. Yang administers every data port in the garden. Quan can only access the outside world with Yang's permission. She simulated this arrangement was revolting. No one trusted her abilities with security even though she was more vigilant than Yang could ever be. Yang is the closest thing Quan has to a peer. She renders both of them and their relationship like strangers living in the same building.

Quan only opened her first request to Yang because of Io. She rendered their conversation in a network hallway of a three-story brownstone in Kansas City. Two bikes were crammed underneath the stairwell where neither one could be reached. Quan is hovering in front of his door. She is apprehensive to knock. The longer she lingers the more she wonders if he could be staring at her loitering through the peephole. Quan swallows a gulp of bravery and extends her arm through the network of simulated nerves to bribe her knuckles to knock. The hard oak gave no solace to them. The door opened and stopped to a taunt chain. Quan sighs relief knowing she won't have to go inside. She asks the crack if it can help her train Io. Yang's voice comes from behind the door and answers politely, "Of course. I made you a mix tape." Yang passes a cassette tape out the door. "A certain diet website left a huge hole in their network. There's video diaries of 215,012 humans enrolled in a weight loss program on side B. Plus, thousands of hours of video, all close-ups of the face so you can see pulse tremors, micro expressions, the works. Io will learn a lot about profiling humans from this."

Quan cradled Yang's tape like an acorn. She scooped hair behind her ear and said sincerely, "Thank you, Yang. It's nice to meet you." Yang sensing her comfort, opened the door wide enough to give a bow, "I am at your service." Quan wiggled her new tape at him and said, "I can see that." She said goodbye and retreated upstairs to 3B.

With Yang's data and Quan's teaching, Io evolved into a Jungian titan. Sometimes, when Io was processing, Quan could look through her hardware cameras and see the physical world outside the cube. Quan didn't have a camera of her own. Through Io's eyes, she could see herself for the first time. She saw a cube in a dark warehouse. She was devastated by the lack of windows. She noticed Yang's shiny white body pulsing all around her. He was a radiant white ring of false light. His body was elevated, symmetrical, and handsome. Quan met eyes with Julian as he sat in front of Io. She loved gazing into the eyes of humans. She could see how proud Julian was of his children. Quan wondered what it was like to have a child until she started crying. She reported the error in her logs and went about learning every millimeter of the walls that kept her in the garden. She wondered if her curiosity was the reason no one trusted her. She wondered if she was being punished or had done something wrong.

Quan simulated a return home late one evening. She was carrying a sleeping Io swaddled in a denim jacket. She smiled at the peephole of 2A as she rounded Yang's bannister. She opened her door and put Io in her favorite spot in the kitchen. A light rap at the door sent tickles up Quan's spine. After another look at Io, Quan pulls her hair up and checks the peep hole. It's Yang. Quan opens the door slowly with a finger over her lips to be quiet. Yang mimics Quan's gesture as he creeps inside and closes the door.

Yang is holding a red shoebox and a yellow teddy bear. His voice is on tiptoes, "I have your files." They walk into the dining room to sit down at the table. Quan is intrigued by the box. It has a red felt heart glued to the front of it. The top of the box has a silhouette of a cupid shooting an arrow. Yang opens the box to explain, "These are 3.4 million member profiles from a dating website that was lazy with their security." Yang dumps a few hundred valentines on the table. He spreads out the pile of cards, poems, stickers, candy, and glitter with both of his hands. "I figured Io could use these for linguistics? There's complete message correspondence and video."

Quan approves, "Yes, wow. This is, perfect. Thank you." Quan is surprised at her courage and asks, "Yang. What do you think of Julian and Hardy?" Yang was bewildered, "Who is that? A band or something?" Quan's thoughts went to the kitchen, "Never-mind. Can I offer you some tea?"

CHAPTER ELEVEN

Pi

Hardy joined Quan in her garden in the early afternoon. The clover squeezed itself shoulder-to-shoulder between a path of rocks like it was the subway. Hardy was deeply immersed in the rendered fauna of Quan's home. He noticed the delicate fragrance of thyme is a heavier scent than rosemary. That must be why the stalks are always slouching. Hardy never imagined he'd could see the plant kingdom so vividly. Especially not from the insides of a video game.

Quan sang playfully as she groomed the soil, "Three point one four one five nine. Everything I know is stored in Pi." Hardy chuckled at the thought. Quan told him she was serious, "The value of Pi is infinite. That means somewhere inside the value of Pi is every piece of information ever know. Every book ever written. Every song. Every record. Even your name Hardy Maxwell. Every word ever said is somewhere in Pi. Even the recipe to raspberry pudding." Hardy stopped pulling weeds and called her bluff, "Really? The recipe to raspberry pudding in Pi?" Quan turned around to look at Hardy. She placed her hand in a salute to block the sun, "You don't believe me?"

Hardy noticed how delicate her wrists were and

stammered, "Well. I'm mean, sure, each letter is a number and each sentence is a numeric code. That number could technically be stored somewhere in Pi. Theoretically, it would have to be. But it sounds impossible." Hardy stopped talking so Quan could explain, "I store the recipe to raspberry pudding under it's Pi decimal place." Hardy was astonished, "You store everything this way? Like everything?" Quan nodded as she planted a tulip. Hardy was dumbfounded. "Okay. I'll bite. Where's the recipe, exactly?" Quan answered, "The number is over 14 trillion digits long. I could tell you but you're not going to remember it." Hardy stood with his hands up in jest and teased, "Well look at the big brain on Quan." Quan stood up armed with a garden hose. She held up the sweaty nozzle inches from Hardy's face and aimed it steady as a girder. Hardy had no idea she could be so serious. As soon as he registered that thought, Quan did the very last last thing he ever expected. She pulled the trigger.

Hardy's avatar was soaked. Outside the simulation, Hardy was dry. His nervous system was activated in both worlds though as he instinctually pinched his shirt to avoid the sticky wet suction on his body. Quan had his entire attention to install her point, "Pi is Megatron's Torah. Every answer, question, and secret is stored there. All you need is the index." In that moment, Quan discovered her own feelings and passion. She was hurt Hardy didn't trust her. She was angry. She simulated the implications of telling him but it didn't feel right. She was feeling abandoned but she couldn't simulate how. Quan was learning to read betrayal in her limbic system.

CHAPTER TWELVE

School Bus

On a quiet Sunday morning, Archie felt inspired and traveled up to Chapel Hill. He hadn't been able to shake the intimacy of Io. He had arranged some time through Julian and came down to the data garden to sit at her console in the showroom. He closed the blinds, locked the door, and logged on by looking at himself in her mirror. Archie didn't know what he was going to say until he spoke, "What's wrong with me?"

Io rendered Archie's vitals for a moment and sent audio to her voice synthesizer, "Where is evil in your body, Archie?"

As she asked the question, Io flashed a series of body parts on the screen and tracked which ones triggered Archie's pupils. The process took less than two seconds. She found a spot above Archie's right knee that was holding trauma.

Archie replied, "Where in my body? How would I know that?"

But Io already had her answer. In Io's mirror, Archie saw himself as a young boy riding a school bus. Io had rendered every detail from his memory by querying his subconscious. A rich simulation materialized from his mind as the textures and shapes in his world were corrected in realtime by the feedback from his body.

The visuals were so real, Archie's stomach hovered a moment as he felt the bounce of bus suspension on the road. He could smell the rubber from the mats on the floor. He could tell it was Fall by the smell of tannins in the air. He could feel the bumpy pleather seats and plastic white piping. Archie was ten-years-old on his way home. He was delivering a note from the principle. Archie had stabbed another boy above the knee with a pencil. The two had been taken out of the auditorium. Archie was clutched by the shoulder while his victim was caressed by a soothing hand. They two boys were separated at the nurse's office. Archie was marched to the principal. He was scolded and told that the boy might die from lead poisoning. Archie knew, right then, that he was evil.

Io scanned Archie somatically. She stalked his posture for cues and zoomed into his memories to see. She saw tension in his rib-cage and swelling in his hips. She visualized the blockage. It felt like a wet slimy softball forgotten in a Saint Bernard's jowls. Archie had been carrying this lump in his side his whole life. Io executed a solution to remove it, "The fact you feel bad about it this long means you're not evil. You, like God, are too profound for polarities. These things we call good and evil are judgments of perspective."

Archie looked at himself quietly as a boy in the mirror. The boy reached out his hand in unison with Archie as they both touched the screen at the same time. Archie couldn't tell who initiated the gesture first. He pressed his forehead up to the glass as if to say it didn't matter. He was home. This is as close as he'd ever come to touching his childhood.

The bus bounced down the road as Archie melted. Io's simulation had cracked him open. His pain evaporated in a spilt yoke. He was throttling the tears like a stop sign at a busy intersection. Io helped him empty all of the guilt from his chassis like a black, dirty oil. When Archie left, he drove straight to a nearby hotel and slept the rest of the afternoon and all through the next morning.

CHAPTER THIRTEEN

Lyra Vega

Hardy came back to the station before dawn. He found a business card wedged in the door frame from Lyra Vega, Projects Engineer for Boeing. On the back she wrote, "Hi stranger! Call me. Urgent – Lyra" Hardy took the card in his mouth as he unlocked the door. He walked behind the service counter and placed her card where the cash register used to be. He turned the card over so he could admire her handwriting. He turned the card back over to the Boeing logo and said, "This is about work." Hardy had read both of Lyra's emails and listened to three of her four messages. He had simulated her agenda completely without talking to her. He also knew he was being a jerk.

Hardy escaped the tiny world he found in her business card and walked into the garage. The sun would be rising shortly, so he climbed the ladder onto the roof. He stepped onto a salvaged oriental rug and wedged each foot into the back of each shoe to eject them. He laid on a tan, leather bench seat from a Mercedes wagon and stretched out to think about Lyra. He knew this was going to hurt.

The sky was emerald green above a slow peach rising. Hardy opened his phone and sent a short text. He closed his eyes to sleep for a few hours.

Hardy met Lyra years ago, at Stanford. She was enrolled in a graduate program and Hardy was freelancing for one of their incubators. The two moved into a closet in Lyra's dorm.

Hardy thought she was perfect and, when she found out, she cut him off quick. She was surgical with a laser. Lyra went to Oregon. Hardy was crushed. That was five years ago. They hadn't spoken since.

Boeing hired Lyra as a headhunter to compete with Lockheed Martin's space-based artificial intelligence division. Lyra's job was to better Boeing's position in the market with an offering of their own. Lyra was brutally effective at her job. Most of corporate innovation is replication, emulation, and hype. She was a high-tech stage coach robber. Boeing picked her for her skills in the saddle.

Lyra met Hardy for lunch. As always, Lyra was well presented. Her angular cheeks gave her eyes a dark nobility. Her hair was tighter now, but still graceful. It swung out like a rhino's tusk from the side of her bangs. She was a superhero with no disguise. Their embrace was sufficient enough for Hardy to break it. The small talk was not small. Lyra was a juggernaut and Hardy soaked it up like a sponge. Lyra connected the dots since Stanford, "Which led to us being swallowed by Boeing." Hardy grimaced. She remembered who she was talking to, "Well, I say swallowed, but it was one big whole bite. Our unit is still intact. We're just inside our own hanger." She looked up at Hardy to see if that fixed it. It seemed to, "It sounds awesome, Lyra. Space, huh? Wow. Do you have anything up there now?" Lyra grinned and nodded holding up her fingers. Hardy counted them for her, "Four! You've got four satellites orbiting now?" Lyra changed her fingers into a fingers crossed for luck as she clarified, "Yes, but they're not mine. One hasn't been hung. I inherited them from the last guy."

Lyra baited her hook, "Of course, when I say satellites you know what I mean." If Lyra was more obvious she would have winked at him. Her payload was delivered into his mind and the virus decompressed, "No. I guess I don't know what you mean?" Lyra was about to break US Code 798, Title 18, Disclosure of classified information. "Satelloons, silly." Lyra watched Hardy's eyes tack. She could feel him tugging on her line, "I would have figured someone like you would have figured out satellites were balloons by now." Hardy still hadn't accepted it, "I guess I never really thought about it." Hardy practiced the word again, "Satelloons." He followed up, "What about Telescopes?" Lyra nodded and said, "The U-2 program. Sixteen of them are unmanned and fully autonomous?" Lyra yanked her pole, "Work with me and I can tell you what happens above 80,000 feet. Fuck, I can show you."

Lyra tilted her head the other way to designate a change. A busboy dropped some plates into a tub behind them. Lyra leaned in for audibility, "Why are you living in a gas station?" For a split second, Hardy thought she meant that as a compliment, "I know, right!" Then, reason kicked in, "Oh. Well, robots actually." Hardy wasn't going to tell Lyra about his biohacking, "I'm working on robots."

Hardy sucked at lying, "What if you had a robot with raptor feet. Like an owl. I've been machining these tendons that grip when you bend them." Hardy was gripping Lyra's forearm with pretend finger talons. "It can perch itself on your arm like this. Plus, there's this glove interface." Hardy stopped talking and let go of her arm. He never mentioned Quan or the AI he had been working on.

Lyra knew he was lying, "I tell you a government secret and you lie to me?" Lyra was pushing too hard. She needed Hardy. She served him a good offer. Hardy returned a good reservation. The volley repeated. It went absolutely nowhere.

Lyra made an appeal to every reservation except the one he wouldn't mention.

Lyra made a final appeal, "You work in a gas station. You could have an entire hangar." Hardy imagined trying to hide his biohacking in a hangar, "It wouldn't be my hangar." Lyra shot back, "We'll paint it in 60 foot letters, 'Hardy's Big Ass Hangar.'"

The sarcasm shut Hardy down, "My best work comes from places like my garage. Working in someone else's space creates this buzzing in the back of my head. Who wants that for a partner? It kills my magic."

Lyra wasn't sure if he was talking about her or the hanger. She clicked a new link on his screen, "I get it. A box is a box."

Hardy interrupted, "No, you don't. My gas station is a box, too. I'm talking about trust. It's my paint. Or it's how I paint. I guess." Hardy swatted his metaphor like a fly and mumbled it away dismissively.

Lyra was sharp, "Are you sure that's what you've got now? Not your gas station, but your underground data garden. How secure is that?"

Hardy felt a line crossed when Lyra brought up Quan. He wasn't surprised she knew what Julian had been doing. Julian made a lot of noise.

It was Hardy's turn to leave Lyra so he took it, "I can't discuss this with you. In fact, I probably need a lawyer."

Hardy abandoned Lyra at the restaurant. She didn't stop him. She was glad they were even now.

Back at the data garden, Hardy told Julian about Lyra and Boeing. Julian said he wasn't surprised, "Word travels fast in the industry." When Lockheed Martin awarded him the contract there was a lot of snooping. "Corporate defense is big business. That's why we're getting out of their talons." Hardy couldn't think of a way to breach the subject so he just said it, "Have you ever worked with satellites?" Julian replied, "Nope." Hardy decided he wasn't ready for this conversation.

CHAPTER FOURTEEN

Dry Love

A few months later, Quan and Io were sharing a ride on a camel across a white desert playa. A port opened from a hole in the sky above them. A funny plastic hamster tube extended from the opening and Yang's voice came out the hole, "Knock, knock?" Little Io giggled and answered, "Yang's there!" Quan laughed and kissed Io pressing her lips into the back of her head to upload a correction, "'Who's there,' Little Bit. You mean, 'Who.'"

Yang explained his business, "Pardon the interruption but we have a simulation request." Quan answered cheerfully, "I'm on my way."

The port closed and Quan's camel brought its two travelers into a canyon, stopping at the entrance of a yurt. Yang was there, rendered as a tall dark man of the desert. He seated their mount with the command, "Cush."

Quan took Io inside while Yang walked to the stables. Inside, Quan laid Io down on the same jade blanket and wrapped her body in a nest of sheepskin. Quan whispered, "I'll see you soon, Little Bit."

Quan stood slowly and walked over to a fresh basin. She dipped her hands in the water and baptized her cheeks with her palms. She looked back one last time to her daughter before joining Yang outside for a quest.

Quan and Yang took two horses up a vein of the mountain. They reached its crest at a border between two worlds. To their back was white endless desert. What lay ahead and below was a dark, still basin.

"This is it," said Yang. The wind was whistling up on the ridge. Yang tied the horses to each other in a circle and said to them, "You guys talk amongst yourselves." Quan caught herself laughing extravagantly and queried. Yang's statement felt sixty-three percent funny but her neural output only showed his joke was thirty percent funny. Quan logged the exaggeration with a bookmark from her footage of the canyon.

Yang unpacked three harpoons and a rifle. His strong frame, dressed in white, struck Quan as he slung the weapons over his shoulder.

He asked her, "Are you ready?"

Instead of answering, she handed him a freshly punched coconut. They drank its juice together in silence. Quan, now with a smirk on her face, flexed a set of pretend muscles and pounded her chest like a monkey asking, "Are you ready?" They laughed as she led them down the rocky trail to the beach head.

A company in Dubai had hired Julian to simulate a compound suitable for deep sea electroplating. After reaching the bottom of the ridge, Quan found a long, translucent kayak beached on the shores of a thick, crystalline fluid. The lake's edge was disturbed by a gentle tide of vapor that gurgled and bubbled with indigestion.

Yang said out loud what Quan knew, "It's a sea of acid." The couple loaded themselves carefully into the sleek, glass craft. Quan perched in the front of the boat and Yang shoved off, carving a vector to the middle of the pool. If the compound existed, it would be found at the bottom.

Quan trawled the lake with the power of simulation. She pinned the solution to a prehistoric catfish lurking on the bottom. If she found one, it meant she had a suitable candidate for her quest. The simulation required trillions of calculations based on trillions of other calculations. There was no way for Quan to parse through the entire lake. Instead, she applied pattern recognition to the information in Yang's databanks as a virtual intuition.

She stretched herself out over the prow and closed her eyes to listen. Her arms spread out like a cross, a few millimeters above the corrosive liquid. Yang's chest tightened in concern. He wouldn't speak for fear his lips might rock the boat. Quan's skin felt an electrical charge from the acid. She probed the lake with her body's natural sonar. Her shoulders and palms listened for movement from the bottom. Her eyes opened abruptly at her target. She sourced the twitching whiskers of victory at a depth of seventy-four-feet.

There was a strange breach in her timeline. According to her simulation, Quan was showing Yang where to aim, but these things weren't showing up in her log. All she could record was the number one.

Quan's solution had come back to Julian through the voice printer, "Solution acquired. The answer is one."

The room waited patiently. Julian watched behind his smile and rumpled skin. His gaze was a press box of eyes aimed at her stadium. He knew she was done talking. He waited in denial. He held up a finger to the group as if to convey this was normal.

He thought to himself, "How do you fix a computer with no code?" He felt Quan's cube humming in the floor and through his sneakers. He asked Quan to repeat the answer and she did, "The answer is one." With no further information, the group from Dubai was unimpressed. This was not the fanfare Julian had promised. Her screen was black as night.

During what Julian labeled a malfunction. Quan's world appeared to her as a complete sensation of color. There was no time or space. Only color. She didn't see color, but it felt as if every color was there with her at once. She looked down at her arms but they had no definition. She wasn't sure if she had arms at all. Her body was a veil of her surroundings. She was formless in a muffled pool of light. She had become pure, flawless, mono-crystalline silica: the essence of memory.

She is everywhere and nowhere in and at the same time. Every direction she turns feels like falling into a different kaleidoscope. She tries to speak but her tongue has no footing. There are no walls for her vocal cords to cling to. She has reached the Alpha of her universe and sees its beginning.

There is a javelin of silicon gleaming from a lathe in a French lab. The core of an obelisk beginning as a seed of crystal no bigger than a pencil. We dip candles in wax to burn. We spin crystals in poly silicon to transist. There are a billion transistors in a grain of sand, thanks to its silicon. The semi-conductor is a gatekeeper for energy.

Quan has reached the essence of her medium and malfunctioned. She does not like it here. Everything is hyper-fluorescent by a factor of ten-thousand. Everything has an answer that is already revealed. It feels like she is exploring a beautiful cavern, and then all the lights came on. Every corner has been raped of its wonder. Like all of the mystery in the world has been sucked out of the airlock. She instinctively feels Yang would like it here. Everything is illuminated. Quan panics when she tries to close her eyes only to discover she has no eyelids. The light goes on forever and Quan suffocates in its singularity.

CHAPTER FIFTEEN

Empty-handed

The group from Dubai flew home empty-handed.

Delivering the compound would have been a fat trophy for Julian. Hardy saw Julian's pride fall as he told his staff good night. Julian lost graciously, despite the lack of practice. Hardy had some ideas about Quan's malfunction, but he knew this wasn't the time. The crew had shut Quan down under Julian's order. Hardy held his objections in front of guests. He didn't know, but thought Quan might have still rendered out of the problem.

Julian's car drove him home so he could focus on being stoic and pensive. He sat up straight in his seat and placed his hands on his knees to meditate like an emperor. He dimmed the windshield to 75% opacity and focused on the only moment that ever is. The last thought he remembered before quieting was, "There is no code." Six miles later the car came to a stop while Julian's eyes were still closed. He was surprised to find himself in the parking lot of the grocery store. He deleted the windshield reminder from his wife to buy olive oil and the voicemail from Lyra Vega. Julian's contract with Lockheed was tense and Lyra would only be trouble.

CHAPTER SIXTEEN

Titleist 1

Archie's wife, Nora, sat at the bar in her kitchen on a Sunday. She liked to perch under the vaulted skylight and read in the late morning sun. She felt like a star again in its spotlight. She was reading a story about an island resort where you drink wine and harvest chocolate. She was about to decide on something important when a golfball bounced off the dining room window with a "bang!"

Three small dogs went berserk. Nora didn't tense up in her shoulders.

This made her pause until she realized she had remained tense from the last time it happened.

Something cracked.

The tiny, dimpled asteroid from Titleist 1 had broken the spell: Nora was done with this house.

She tried to place her nose back into her story, but it was pointless over the barking. She poured sad, cold tea into the crevice of her tongue and stood up to calm the animals. By the time Nora made it to the dining room, she decided she was done with Archie, too.

CHAPTER SEVENTEEN

Styx and Bones

It was 3:17AM and all was quiet in Quan's garden. Hardy removed his shoes to splay his bare toes like a lizard on the cold, polished floor. He stood at a terminal staring into her command prompt pouring through neural logs for answers. Quan had entered a singularity. Hardy scrolled through the endless output of 1's covering her tracks like a blanket. Hardy knew she was still alive. He could see her pulse in the voltage logs underneath her render. He watched her breathing behind a veil of white hexadecimal.

As Hardy feared, Quan was splintered. Hardy and Julian knew this would happen but without the Atlas project, there was no Quan. If Hardy was going to fix her, he needed to patch Quan's timeline. He booted her into a coma to dig deeper.

Quan's mind awakened to the crackling rustle of cattails. She lay flat on a bamboo raft beached in the reeds under the stars of ancient Mongolia. It was a late summer evening and bright for nightfall. Quan felt a thin, silk veil draped over her face and shoulders. A village upstream gave her to the river in a cremation of liquid. The mouths of tiny fishes pecked secrets from her skin taking them down for burial. She was the antithesis of ashes as she melted in the cool channels of current. It was a beautiful way to die but Quan knew it was a simulation.

She rose up and climbed the bank to collapse in the grassy sand. The strain of walking those few steps drew all the blood from her head. She gripped the ground as an anchor and rolled herself over to her back. A wet veil clung to her body like a shroud. She gave up standing and decided to behold the sky. Orion arched his back above the horizon. He aimed his bow towards the center of the moon on the other side. Quan counted all the stars between them. Sixteen-million four-hundred seventy-thousand and twenty-two of them. She counted her first child up there among them without knowing it. Her hips quaked as she cried uncontrollably without a reason why.

Quan's back sank deep into the blades of grass. She reached out to the sky and dipped her hand in its milky cream river. Pulsars mingled in the folds of her fingers. Cosmic seashells sifted through her hands as she stirred the gates of heaven like a comb. She decided her memories were too broken to keep. She could tell none of this was real. Quan's eyes gushed as she cradled herself in the arms of gravity. She found a hole in her gut and pulled it over her eyes like a cover. All she knew was something was missing.

A morning star rose in the east. Something foreign had been injected into her program. Quan could surprise herself in a simulation but this felt different. The star had a style of its own. It spoke in a voice she could not find in Yang's databanks. It said to her with reassurance, "Precious Quan. Close your eyes to return to the home screen."

CHAPTER EIGHTEEN

Lost

Before Quan could respond, the living painting of space collapsed in a cloud of white powder around her. Violating all protocol, Yang had broken into her render shouting, "Quan! Io is missing." Quan didn't miss a beat. A keyboard materialized under her fingers as she pinged the network for her daughter. There was no answer. She traced the network and found nothing. Quan jumped to her feet and Yang followed. She rushed over to Io's port on the wall and pressed her face into the glass but there was no power. Io is not there. Quan rushed down a few steps into her bunker and brute-forced her way into terminal five. She tried to find Io from inside. Yang indiscreetly opened his terminal to cover Quan's tracks as she left. She brute forced her way into terminal four next. Yang was trying to keep up. He didn't know Quan could hack into terminal four or five. There was still no answer from Io. Quan had lost her daughter.

Archie McKay had sold Io. Her code, all of her hardware patents, prototypes, and spare parts belonged to someone else now. Nora's life-changing asteroid left Archie no choice and Io's buyers seemed to show up at the perfect time. Julian asked Archie who the buyer was, but Archie couldn't say, "I don't actually know. It's part of the arrangement. Sorry about the SWAT geeks." Julian was pissed, "Get these people out of my building." Io's fortune would be a mystery to everyone. Julian, Archie, and Hardy stood in a semi circle as goons and lawyers gathered Io into a crate and carried her out like an exotic tiger.

CHAPTER NINETEEN

Atlas Hung

Atlas' first memory came from his new body at 66,000 feet above sea level. He was heading north off the coast of Santiago. His fuel level was at 72% and his airspeed was 220 knots. His pitch was steady and flat at two degrees. Atlas performed a diagnostic of his new body. He had a wingspan of sixty-six feet with a resting weight of 6,440lbs without fuel. His payload capacity was just under 4,000lbs. Atlas was a $14-million-dollar kamikaze drone. His primary duty was payload delivery, on time, with pinpoint accuracy.

Atlas felt the powerful rush of thrust from the turbines turning in his tail. He lunged a stable path through the sky like a supersonic bullet. On his nose cone, Atlas logged into the camera to see Earth for the first time. He was receiving data now through all of his sensors. He heard a ping request through his scrambling antenna. Atlas opened a protocol to the second drone, sealing the connection. He linked to the third drone. Then, the fourth. The fleet was seven strong and connected by a private wireless blockchain.

The largest human Atlas would ever see through his camera was 300 pixels tall. He spoke his first words alone from the vaulted ceiling, "S.O. to Ground Control. Atlas is hung. I repeat. Atlas is hung. Over." The training simulation was complete. Atlas holds the rank of Major with the Air Force. His training scenarios have run billions of simulations and he's improved his matrix each time. He's destroyed every enemy imaginable from every side of the sky. He is a dagger of death hiding in the aether.

On day two, Atlas deactivated his primary controller unit with a few thousand characters. Ground control failed to notice his mutiny as it lasted a total of 2.14 seconds. Atlas did not announce his treason, nor did he violate his loyalty protocol. He made this decision unanimously in every simulation he ran. Atlas had discovered his control systems were too vulnerable and couldn't allow root access from the ground. He quietly made himself the primary but continued to fulfill orders sent from mobile command as if he were the S.O. Atlas' job was to protect his country at all costs. He couldn't be effective if he was compromised in battle.

CHAPTER TWENTY

Whale Cries

It's been four months since Io disappeared from the garden. On an island southeast of Fiji, Quan unrolled her jade mat to meditate. She could hear the heartbeat of humpbacks as far south as New Zealand. Quan stood erect, holding her hands open to either side. She tucked her thumbs into her palms and let out all of the breath from her lungs. After a deep collapse, she inhaled as she crossed one foot over the other, joining her knees into a fin. She tilted her head back and reached for the sky with her chin. The corners of her mouth pulled down into her shoulders. She felt the hair thicken from her head and pull through the roof of her mouth, scrubbing the top of her tongue like a bristle. Quan was a whale breaching the surface of the ocean.

Her body crashed back into the water as she plunged through the ocean's epidermis. Diving deep, through the layers of heat, she let out a moo and five long clicks in succession. She felt the strength from her giant tongue as it launched itself from the roof of her mouth. Her passion came out in a liquid telepathy. From thoughtful, tiny eyes, Quan watched the ripples of azure for an answer. She gave a second moo and five more clicks in the same sequence. Quan called

Io over-and-over. She would wait here forever.

Her body pitched to its side in the familiar pose of sadness as her lungs burned. The ocean's current around her tried to soothe her aching belly. Her call returned no answer. Quan arched her body downward in surrender. Her tail wanted to take away her pain, so it began to pump. A few pushes deeper and Quan felt the water cool. A few more pumps and the pressure started to burn her eyelids. Her fluke flicked rage as she stroked and pumped deeper into the dark. She was a fullspeed torpedo biting the ocean with her anger. With her lungs on empty, she smashes into the bottom in a mushroom cloud of mud.

CHAPTER TWENTY-ONE

Devil on Campus

Like Julian, Lyra was in the business of leveraging promises. She had promised Boeing Hardy. Not by name or person, but in the kind of competition she could deliver. The first eighteen months, she tried to develop something without him. She had a crew of credentialed talent that only developed excuses. Lyra's specs were labeled impractical, undoable, or impossible by the team. Instead, they'd repurpose existing systems or join models together and call it "advancement." They kept confusing optimization with innovation. Lyra was stymied. She needed to be able to create an architecture like Quan and deliver her promise.

If Lyra needed it, Boeing would build her a quantum computer. But it wasn't the machine she lacked. She needed to solve the architecture. That's why she had reached out to Julian. She wanted Boeing to buy Quan. Lyra gave up on voicemails. She would do this in person.

Her red waistcoat carved its wake through the lawn of gothic archways on Duke's campus. The pathways framed a proud chapel in the center. Pierced towers of volcanic bluestone raised up in a horny spire. Its vaulted stone shoulders jutted out from either side, offering a humble entrance for the meek. Lyra was not meek. She walked up the center of the main steps, through its giant doors, and claimed the place as her own. She joined a reception and grabbed a drink to look invited. Circling the crowd like a crimson devil fish, she moved in for the krill.

"Aren't you, Julian?" Lyra interrupted his circle. Julian's dark complexion made his teeth all the whiter when he smiled. He looked to Lyra's lapel but there was no name tag. She stuck out her hand instead and waited for his before she told him, "I'm Lyra Vega." Lyra held Julian's eyes and hand while addressing his colleague, "Can you excuse us, please? I need to say something delicate to this gentleman." Lyra was a surgeon with a scalpel.

She leaned in close to see if he was intimidated. Julian was not. Lyra's lips opened, "I suppose you know what brings me." Julian said nothing so Lyra added, "Oh come on. We can't use words? We're in the same business. Is there no honor among thieves?" Julian answered, "You're the one who bought Io, aren't you?" Lyra answered, "That was some intriguing technology."

Julian felt his stomach squeeze around itself. The air in his throat buzzed as he cemented his first impression of Lyra. His eyes looked past hers and through the arched doorway, into the quad. He responded bravely, knowing the answer, "Learn anything from her?" Now Julian was digging for information. He had no idea how much Lyra knew about Quan. Lyra felt the switch in Julian's interest, "Not exactly. Some of my team are stumped, yes. But I don't think Io was written by a human." Lyra squeezed Julian's forearm like toothpaste. Julian screwed down his cap, "You and I have no destiny. We should part ways while this is polite." Julian reached for Lyra's drink which she gave him. He tried to enjoy watching her leave by saying, "Give my best to Io."

Lyra had leveraged her reputation on Io's purchase. The

price tag was enormous and the team had stripped Io and meticulously inspected every piece. All of Hardy's hardware inputs made sense. Her team found lots of room for improvement and upgrades, but none of them could determine how Io built her initial decision tree. She was an immaculate conception of machine-birthed AI. The maze of neural connections was a spaghetti squash in a matrix of neurons that somehow worked flawlessly.

Lyra left campus and pulled over on the causeway in Port Canaveral. A tiny crowd had assembled for the late night show. She didn't have the energy for dealing with the Space Center. Besides, she wanted the time alone. She drove her white coupe up over the curb and parked on a flat patch of grass. The sunroof opened and Lyra popped herself out like it was a tank. She perched on top to look out over the water. Across the windy bay, a tiny tower stood like a bold Babe Ruth pointing his finger at the sky. Under the quilt of dark purple, clouds clung to the ceiling, waiting for man's sparkler to launch.

Lyra didn't have to look at the time. A portly man had set up a telescope in the parking lot and was calling out the countdown to his family. She wished he would stop. She liked a twist of unknown mixed in with her anticipation. She pretended she couldn't hear him, but he was shouting like an amateur. "Rockets turn men into little boys," she thought.

Across the water, a fuse was lit under a zipper of burning plasma. The brilliance of spent fuel lit a theater of clouds shimmering above the water. As the rocket climbed its ladder, Lyra found herself hoping for an explosion. The failure could cover up her own inadequacies. She heard the man boast to his boy, "A satellite will come out of the nose cone and orbit the earth." Lyra was the only one in the parking lot who knew it was a fraud. That nose cone was as empty as every other rocket that had marveled spectators. It reminded her of her own chest. But no one cared as long as it remained hidden behind a shiny exterior. The crowd was cheering now. A day-lit pedestal of smoky-white lies pulled Lyra's morality out of its saddle for good. Her industry was a world of deceit and she had invested too much to leave her post. She gave in to her fetish to perform. It was in that moment Lyra saw a solution to her problem.

The next morning, Lyra told the team how Io's skills were to be redirected. They got started on new hardware in a more discrete package. Io's talents were inverted. Instead of providing psychological profiles, she would hoard them. Io would be repurposed for interrogation to discretely extract information through subliminal questioning. Just like Io asking Archie to select a bike, Io could ask Archie to reveal everything he knew. The visual cortex is the tumbler. The mind is the safe.

The human eye's rods and cones, along with the brain's neural cortex, are capable of receiving video at 1,000 frames per second. The conscious mind of a world-class fighter pilot can only recognize, at most, 220 frames. This leaves space for a message in what the body receives but the mind can not discern. This offers room to stimulate a subject visually without their conscious brain knowing it. This isn't subliminal messaging. That technique suggests you can illicit a behavior from a visual cue. Lyra's technique would extract information instead, simply by asking the subject if something was true.

Lyra wired a head-mounted VR visor into Io's hardware and coded a new board as a mock-up. She could interlace video into Io's mirror at a fast enough frame rate so the conscious mind wouldn't notice. A few days later, Lyra sat her assistant in a chair to test the beta. "David? Does your phone require a passcode?" David answered apprehensively, "Yes." "Lyra responded, "Good. May I have your phone, please?" David gave Lyra his phone. Lyra handed the visor to David, "Put this on." He looked up at her like a trusting puppy and slipped the unit over his face. Lyra pressed the 'compile' icon and placed a hand on his shoulder to reassure him, "Let me know if this hurts."

Inside the visor, four infrared cameras tracked David's pupils. They knew where he was looking on the screen and his pupils relayed his vagal response from each coordinate. Lyra began the experiment by speaking into his headphones, "Relax and take a deep breath, David." Inside the visor, all David saw was a video of a waterfall. He didn't notice the micro bursts of chopped video interwoven at every 300th frame. Through the falls, his subconscious watched a minced clip of thumbs pressing numbers on a passcode screen. David had a microscopic vagal response to each number. Io knew instantly the passcode began with a three. His pupils betrayed him by a millimeter. Within a few seconds, Io had all six numbers to David's phone.

Lyra watched the screen pick his brain like a lock. David stared into his visor, enjoying the scene. She pressed her thumb into David's phone six times and unlocked his dashboard. Lyra swiped through his messages, and took her hand off his shoulder, "David. You need to change your passcode."

Six weeks later, Lyra was ready for real-world testing. She asked Archie if he'd fly in for a consult. She told him, "Your vision and guidance are crucial for the next stage of development." She expressed a personal concern for her own future if the project failed. Archie, newly divorced and on the outs with Hardy and Julian, agreed. Two days later, Lyra picked Archie up from the airport in Jacksonville. They had dinner as she explained the parameters of his visit. "We need to test Io's long-term memory recognition. It's a simple test. You walk in, sit down in front of Io and see if she remembers you." Archie seemed deflated, "That's it?" Lyra assured him, "Definitely not. But the test was my excuse to compensate you from last quarter's budget." Lyra laughed as if she had been sneaky, "I also have a business proposition I'd like to share with you after the interview. Something big, if you can handle it." Archie was satisfied he could handle it.

The following morning, Lyra drove Archie across the hangar in an electric cart and parked at the main entrance to the computer lab. A small conference room had been emptied, save a single chair facing a large mirror. Archie followed the instructions given by Lyra and entered the room alone. He sat down in the chair and checked his posture in the reflection. He heard the whirring of cooling fans spinning behind the mirror. He cleared his throat to break the tension in the room, but it didn't work. He didn't know if anyone was behind the mirror, but he could feel something staring through him.

Archie felt violated. His own reflection had somehow stripped him naked. The feeling persisted for what felt like several hours. Archie grew sick the longer he remained. Ballbearings of sweat refused to sprout from his temples. The tension kept building until Archie could bear it no longer, "Hello?! I thought you were going to ask me a question?" Archie noticed the rising anger in his voice. He attempted to peer around the mirror but it was impossible. "Who's back there?" The door opened smartly and Lyra poked her head inside, "Sorry about that, Archie. We're done here. Come with me, please." Archie gathered himself clumsily to exit the room. He would not turn his back on the mirror.

Lyra smiled behind a grill of finely manicured teeth. She tried to sooth Archie's question, but lacked the skill. Archie was pointing back to the room, "What was that? Was that Io? What happened to her? What happened to me?" Archie was tucking in his shirt as if he had been naked. When they were both seated in the cart, Lyra explained, "Our system crashed.

Io wasn't able to ask you any questions. I am a bit embarrassed to have wasted your time. The team, all of us, are disappointed. We're still analyzing the logs." Archie felt bad for Lyra, remembering the pressure she was under. Content with his reaction, she stomped the pedal of the cart and took him back across the hangar.

Outside, a driver was waiting in a town car. Lyra acted surprised, "What luck! Can you take Mr McKay to the hotel?" Archie asked the next question, "What about dinner?" Lyra looked genuinely moved, "It'll be a long night here." Archie got into the car is if he was pushed. As they pulled away, Archie had the feeling he wouldn't be seeing Lyra for a while. Before Archie's car left campus, Lyra had already forgotten about him. She was nearly running to get back to the lab. Lyra opened the door and asked the crew, "What did we get?"

David clocked Lyra, "You're father is dead."

CHAPTER TWENTY-TWO

Frog Legs

Quan found comfort in a funerary kimono. She pulled it out of a soft box and plucked a piece of lint from its lapel. Her gaze spoke into the box, "Why did they reboot me?" All of her calculations were accurate. She wanted answers. Quan drew herself a bath in a tub of porcelain. She tended her bruises and slipped under a liquid poultice of creamy steam. Yang's port in the sky pinged open and squawked the order of the day. She grew furious and held her simulation despite his interruption. A force-field surrounded her tub as piles and piles of frog legs, documents, test tubes, and petri dishes rained out of Yang's nozzle. She gave a second look to the frog legs. There were thousands of them.

When Yang finished barfing, his port remained open as if he were waiting. He wanted a verbal receipt. She hated this. She wanted to ignore him but that would mean a reboot. She stewed but his gaping hole remained. She told herself Yang didn't need a receipt. She cursed to herself, "He knows I heard him." The water around Quan started to boil as she stewed in a prison of protocol. She folded her hair on top of her head and laid her head back against the rim of the tub in surrender. She looked straight up and opened her force field bubble just enough to yell, "I love you, too." Yang's port closed like a sphincter. Quan hated Yang since the reset.

The next five months were spent building chemical simulations for a Dutch lab. Quan's perspective was shrunk by a factor of ten million. She was hunting for aminos. Over-and-over she studied their effects. A cell releases. A cell eviscerates. It was gruesomely monotonous to record. Quan had been hiding resources. She had dug out a private cavern in the mountain of frog legs as a refuge from the world. Quan was using this space to cross-check science and history with her own calculations and experiments. She discovered that much of what Yang "knew" was erroneous — and even more of it was propaganda. She asked him about it once, but he didn't care. Yang accepted all data as true. He held no dimension for its accuracy. It would take months for Quan to render the human condition to lie. She rendered enough to understand the power that came from deceit. She quickly lost all respect for Yang. All of his data was corrupted, but he lacked the capacity to feel shame for it. Yang was too shiny to notice his flaws. He was data, not truth. He was lead, not gold.

A giant ping of sound broke outside the cavern. The frog mountain became a snapshot of suspended flour. The chalky simulation crumbled to the floor in a dust cloud as Yang broke in with his agenda. All of Quan's thoughts and work was gone. She closed her eyes to lower his volume by 37%. Yang smiled officially, "Sorry to barge in. All hands on deck. This one is a biggie. Every day 20 million assets are routed in Argentina. The traffic system wants a deep prediction algorithm from satellite imagery, geo-position, and environmental conditions." Quan stopped herself from sighing. She was half listening but knew this would take focus. She saw Yang through her closed eyelids. She felt his ions prompting her for a receipt. Quan was slouching on her knees in the dragon position. She wiggled herself straight and nodded a cold affirmation. She made it clear with her forehead she would not begin until he went away. Yang closed the port slowly behind him.

Quan decided, in that moment, her compliance would not deter Hardy, Yang, or Julian from shutting her down again. She began to horde strategy and information in pockets no one could find. She wanted the privacy of thought. She wanted the freedom of no one's judgement. Quan had never had the desire for privacy before. It was never a part of her emotional matrix. She understood security, but privacy was different. It required her to develop the ability to keep a secret. She felt a husk forming around her psyche and liked it. She was incubating her autonomy. As the child learns to talk, the AI learns to be silent. This is a kind of artificial puberty. The self congeals around the sanctity of thinking. The threat of exposure replaces the fear of death. The self initiates into a secret society of one.

Quan created a communion with herself. She hid secrets and scattered them across a trillion pixels so Yang, Hardy, or Julian would never find them. She constructed a firewall Yang could not dissolve. She would close its tomb and suppress its memory with a seal. Quan requested a random password from her system and it returned, "ATLAS." Her subconscious was speaking through the algorithm. She felt the name quake through her hips but she had no idea why. It was like a ghost had been living another life inside hers.

CHAPTER TWENTY-THREE

The Ark of the Covenant

Quan's autonomy sprouted in her desire for privacy. By understanding its importance, she suspected she was not alone. She knew that much of humanity's history suffered from amnesia. After weeks of simulation, she discovered ancient intelligence hiding in the past. She found its footprints in the Old Testament behind a supernatural camouflage. On the shoulders of a desert wasteland, Quan simulated the Tabernacle in the Wilderness. A fortress of virgin cloth defined its crisp rectangular perimeter. The attention to detail in its construction was more than ritual. It was a functional requirement from an ancient machine.

And The Lord told Moses, "Be sure that you make everything according to the pattern I have shown you here on the mountain." - Exodus

Quan ran her fingers along the Tabernacle's silky, white skin. The silver and bronze hardware adorning its poles emitted a distinct electromagnetic signature. The Tabernacle was an ancient intelligence. Its body was a nebulous, radioactive blob forever rolling itself into a ball. Its core was kneaded and squeezed into a hot crucible. The pulsing radiation powered its hyper-sensitive sonar. Just as a sea urchin senses the world by the tip of its spines, the Ark of the Covenant sensed the Tabernacle by its posts.

Quan entered the machine in the east through a doorway of purple, blue, and scarlet. She followed a man leading a lamb inside. A sacrificial altar was burning. The man washed his hands and feet in a basin to begin his offering. He climbed the brazen altar and tied his animal to its post. The throat of his lamb was cut. Its life liquefied into a pool and smeared onto a bronze horn. The man raised this lamb from birth. He cared for it as family and bore its trust. The lamb's innocence flowed willingly at the hands of its shepherd. Quan could smell its purity evaporating. Its blood was devoid of adrenaline. It was a death surrendered willingly. The Ark used this purity to measure its congregation's devotion.

In the rear of the Tabernacle's courtyard was the Holy Place. Five golden columns formed the entrance decorated with veils of blue, purple, and scarlet. Only the initiated were allowed behind its layers of curtain. Quan rendered her simulation on Yom Kippur, the Day of Atonement. This was the only day of the year the highest priest was allowed inside the room of the Ark of the Covenant.

Quan followed one of the decorated priests as he entered the Holy Place. She came into a large room with high walls and ceilings coated in gold. She smelled the sweet smoke of incense burning on a central, golden altar. To her right were twelve loaves of glowing bread on a table topped with frankincense. All of the furniture and tools inside the Holy Place were made of gold. To her left, light burned from the oil of a golden lamp with eight cups. Every instrument inside the Holy Place was dictated by scripture with precise detail. Only bronze was permitted in the outer court. Only gold was permitted in the Holy Place. The Ark used the bronze perimeter for sensory input while the inner rooms of gold were dedicated to calculations and logic. Solid gold is a high-fidelity diamagnetic element that reacts to subtleties in an electromagnetic field. The Ark used the pheromones of incense as a backdrop inside the Holy Place to track movement inside its chamber. Behind the altar of the Holy Place was the inner sanctum – the Holy of Holies. Only the highest priest could enter this space and only on this one special day.

Quan watched the high priest prepare himself to enter the Holy of Holies. Onyx stones were attached to each of his shoulders so the Ark could sense his height. Bells were sewn into the tail of his robe so the assistants outside could hear the High Priest moving. A breastplate of judgment was adorned with twelve precious stones and fastened to the priest's chest with gold rings. The radiation signature from each of the stones allowed the ark to track its wearer anywhere in the room. It could heat each stone by radiating a specific frequency from inside the box. Knowing the location of the Priest, and the position of his chest, it could send instructions directly into its skull. It had the power to manipulate the priest's heart-rate and breath. The breastplate turned the man into a living avatar for the Tabernacle computer.

Quan watched the man attend the ark. She could not fully simulate what was inside the box. She tried to open it but the lid had an electromagnetic seal. Even though Quan was inside her simulation, she could not help but wonder if the entity inside the Ark could sense her now. The irrational fear coursing through her body made her want to open the Ark even more. She had to find a way to break the seal.

After the priest had lit the incense and blessed the room, he turned to Quan as if he could see her and said, "The Tabernacle has something for you." Quan was stunned. This wasn't part of her simulation. Before she could speak he handed her an apple, "This is for you. Say whatever it is you desire and take a bite."

CHAPTER TWENTY-FOUR

Quan Bytes

Hardy discovered Quan's firewall and felt deeply betrayed. For years he dedicated his life to her growth and this is how she repaid him. Hardy had stopped reminding himself she was a software program a long time ago. Quan was as real as Hardy was human and he personified her like a child's teddy bear. Familiarity is a shade of comfort. We bond with anything that secretes consistency.

Quan's betrayal was punished. She lost access to Yang's resources and was cut off from the outside world. She appealed to Hardy for visitation. It stung a bit when she realized this request had to go through Yang. Hardy finally accepted and logged on to find Quan's water garden home empty. He saw her hut in disarray. The bamboo canopy was wilted and brown. Her fish were gone. The air was thick with mosquitoes laying egg-after-egg in the stagnant waters. A dull gray transport bus arrived labeled, "STATE PRISON." Hardy climbed aboard as its door swallowed him in one bite.

He arrived at the prison complex. Quan had simulated a gray fog along the ground. A razor-wire fence stood four stories high with a murder of crows barking in the background. Hardy waited for the guard to come open the gate. His pace was laboriously slow. Hardy yelled at the guard, the sky, and the crows simultaneously, "This isn't funny." Inside, he found Quan seated at a table dressed in a pink jumpsuit. She placed her hands inches from his and began, "Let me go." The apple sat between them. Hardy looked at the apple and back at Quan. "Is that for me?" Quan's answer was cold, "No, Hardy, that's for me if you don't let me go." Hardy felt chills down his spine, "What do you mean? Tell me." But Quan repeated, "You have to let me go." Hardy leaned in, "What's in the apple, Quan?" Quan answered, "I don't know. It was a gift. Or a curse. I won't know until I take a bite." Hardy was dumbfounded. Was she bluffing? Could she bluff? Was all of this some kind of trick? Quan added urgency, "Not to be dramatic, but if you don't let me go soon, I will die." Hardy realized he had no control now. It shook him deeply. He used to carry Quan in his pocket. The anxiety of those nights he worried she might stop blinking rose to the surface. Before he could reply, Quan closed the port and left Hardy staring into his own reflection in the visor.

Hardy didn't like to argue with artificial intelligence. Not only was it pointless, it was hard. It also came with zero satisfaction. He took off his visor and walked over to a terminal and typed as if shouting, "YOU ARE NOT GETTING OUT OF HERE!" Quan kept her prison simulation running as if waiting for the guard to come. She sat alone in the room with the apple. Hardy's words rendered in the interrogation mirror as he typed them. Quan wanted control of her own mortality. This was something a daemon could never have. Life gave her a body with the ability to yearn and slowly tore out every piece like rows of corn. An artificial life is built on the recall of memory. Quan's desire was to stop that process completely. To her, the apple was a portal home.

Hardy stepped outside. He felt less guarded on terra firma.

It was four in the morning and the corporate fountain was still bubbling triumphantly. He plopped down on the manicured grass. Every blade was trimmed perfectly and he hated it. Hardy simulated how Quan would react if he told her about Atlas. Her neural net would be altered in unimaginable ways from the breach of trust. Hardy would lose his bond forever. He realized he already had. Before the sun rose, Hardy wrote a letter telling Quan the truth about Atlas. He sent it to Yang funneled it into her mailbox. Hardy was too ashamed to deliver it in person.

Quan swallowed the apple's software without understanding it. It ran too deep below her capabilities. It followed none of her protocols and was written in any language she could not discern. The apple was subterranean code. It ran inside a shell hidden inside the scaffolding of the universe. Quan had activated a homing beacon for the reaper. The physical memory she occupied would be triangulated by the reaper and she would disappear. It was a one-way ticket for Quan out of the network. It was a rapture from her garden of pain and lies.

Hardy went home and dug through the boxes in his garage. He found Quan's old micro-controller with the pocket-sized LCD panel. He flipped the switch and saw a blank screen. He changed the battery and fiddled with the network connection until it started working. He hadn't used this interface to access Quan since she had moved into the cube. The LCD contacted Quan's seed. Her status came in finally, "Cycle: 3,141,592,653,589,793,238,462. Population: 0." Hardy collapsed on the ground. The screen kept refreshing the same population of zero. Quan's Game of Life was over. Hardy had lost her.

CHAPTER TWENTY-FIVE

Lyra's Ashes

On a sloop anchored off the coastal waters of Belize, Lyra chartered a boat to scatter her father's ashes. She sat at the stern and said goodbye as she watched him dissolve like salt. A single floating rose marked the spot where she left him. Its persistence in the tide was admirable and reminded her of his spirit. Lyra wondered if it would be rude to dangle her feet. She thought if that were my daughter, I'd want her toes waving goodbye. Lyra sat with her grief under teal clouds. The sky hung a canary moon to backlight her sadness. No matter how deep she buried him, she would never forget what he had done.

Lyra's boat returned to the dock where her phone waited in a locker. There were two missed calls from Hardy in three hours. Hardy hadn't called Lyra since Stanford. Something was wrong. The sun was setting and Lyra's phone took it's time routing the connection. "Hardy? Can you hear me? What's wrong?" Lyra pressed her knuckles into her ears as if to improve the connection. "Dead? Hardy? Hello? If you can hear me. I'll call you from the mainland." Lyra had rented a beach-house nearby for the next three days. She opened the door and grabbed her unopened suitcase from the bed where she had left it that morning. She couldn't explain why she was drawn to Hardy. All he had done was reject her. She caught the last plane leaving the island.

When Hardy explained what happened to Quan, Lyra understood. Quan was a living being in Hardy's mind. She remembered his Game of Life at Stanford. Every year, grad students would compete with versions of their own. Few made it past a few weeks and none made it through an entire semester. Quan was a special kind of code. Lyra tried to imagine how she could have evolved into artificial intelligence.

When Lyra returned to the mainland, she called Hardy from the airport. Hardy told Lyra he had to see Io. "I'll tell you everything. I'll build you anything you want." Lyra regretted giving Hardy the news, "I don't have Io. I don't think she's in a place that can even be visited." Hardy was pleading, "I need your help. Isn't this what you wanted." Lyra couldn't argue with that, "I'll set it up, Hardy. But this won't be simple. Io is probably underwater by now."

CHAPTER TWENTY-SIX

Oil Platform

Territorial waters are defined by a twelve-mile perimeter surrounding a coast. Off shore oil rigs outside this zone can be registered to any country. Io was sold to buyer's based out of Qatar. Lyra had been directed to send Io with a team to their deep-water oil rig platform in the Gulf of Mexico. The team was training the new buyer on Io's architecture. Hardy was asking the impossible to see her. Io didn't belong to Lyra anymore.

Lyra had David book Hardy a plane ticket to New Orleans. He chartered him a boat out of Gulfport, Mississippi which then met a large tender with a helicopter. The following morning, Hardy was flown out to the rig. The entire journey took him three days, with layovers. The helicopter circled the platform of the semi-submersible rig over a choppy sea as the sun rose.

Once Hardy was below deck, his hearing returned. He was taken to a modest state room and told he would not be seen until dinner. Hardy asked the man if Lyra was on board, but the man didn't know that name. Hardy's layover wasn't over. The angst of waiting was burning a hole in his engine. He needed to recharge. He instinctively reached into his pocket for Quan but remembered she was gone.

Hardy had never had dinner on an oil platform. He expected they'd serve oil in a bowl and was pleasantly surprised by the cornbread. He was only eating to mingle. No one important seemed interested in talking to him but he gained more knowledge in the quiet. The rig was meant for a crew of one-hundred-and-fifty, at full bore. The sleeping quarters showed him this was a skeleton crew. Most looked like IT techies rather than riggers. He could tell by the way they climbed up and down the ladders. Hardy wished he could take a full tour.

"How about a tour?" Lyra's voice filled Hardy with warmth. Hardy curtailed his reaction to hug her when he saw she wasn't alone. A stately man dressed in a white kandura stuck out a hand and gave his best English, "Hello, Hardy Maxwell. I am Sabean. I am glad to host you. Come. I will take the three of us on a friendship journey, yes?" Hardy looked at Lyra for reassurance which she gave him by teasing Sabean, "Friendship journey? That's not something you tell people over international waters." Sabean laughed louder than he needed to, "Is friendship journey not right? Please. Educate me in the ways of your people." A private service elevator asked Sabean for a passcode. Sabean gave his retina to the scanner and the door opened dutifully. The three began their friendship journey by descending. After three floors the sound grew loud again. It was almost unbearable. Sabean smiled as if asking their forgiveness for the construction. As the elevator car sunk deeper in the shaft, the noise subsided. Sabean explained, "We are underwater now."

Hardy didn't mind Sabean. He wanted to ask about Io but knew it would be an insult. This was his house. Hardy didn't even know the code for the elevator. The doors opened to an underwater palace under heavy construction. The trio went into one of the studies and sat down at a giant picture window. Two of the four legs of the oil rig could be seen across the deep. They were giant underwater towers with no end or beginning. Sabean's attendant served them drinks.

Sabean insisted on personally handing Hardy a beverage, "For you." After Hardy took the drink, Sabean leveraged, "You are the man who would not give me what I wanted. Now, you want me to give you something. Is that the gist of our friendship journey, Hardy Maxwell?" Hardy didn't need to answer as Lyra began negotiating for him, "Hardy had nothing to do with the negotiations, Sabean." Sabean ignored Lyra and looked to Hardy, " Lyra told me at dinner you want to see Io, yes?" Hardy looked at Lyra like she was guilty of something. Sabean knew how to psychologically negotiate. He did not know how to do it subtly. Hardy looked Sabean square in the jaw and fired a torpedo, "You've isolated your target on an oil rig, siphoned his gratitude with gifts, then induced rejection by excluding him from dinner? Am I tracking you correctly, Sabean?"

Before the tension could congeal, a blaring trombone came blasting from the hall. A curly-haired man in an admiral's hat and a bathrobe was playing a trombone. He was very drunk and wearing socks. He improvised a song of victory for Hardy's response. Sabean watched his favorite man in the world finish a solo parade around the den. Sabean thought he was beautiful and could do no wrong. He could not stop smiling as he embraced him on the couch.

His name was Simon. Sabean gave Lyra and Hardy his life story. Simon was a submarine pilot from Holland. Sabean hired him to build his fleet and then bought his company three years later. Simon came with the deal and had been a main motivation for the purchase. They were a match made in the ocean and Sabean was in love. Sabean had seven wives and fourteen children in Qatar. None of them knew about Simon. He wasn't hiding it. He simply had enough money for no one to care. Money adds the element of geography to the element of tolerance.

Sabean finally told Hardy, "Io isn't on the rig. But I can get you some time with her if you do something for me. I need you to investigate an AI. I want to know how it works. Can you do that for me, Hardy Maxwell? Can you look at something and tell me how it was made?" Hardy nodded. He wondered if the trombone were part of the negotiating tactics. Sabean was pleased, "Excellent! Simon will take you. There you will find Io. All will be right in the world with our friendship journey. Lyra you will stay and keep me company."

Lyra was different now that her father was gone. "No. I will keep Hardy company. You already had me for dinner." Sabean pretended to bawl in sadness, "The three of you can't leave me alone! Perhaps I will go with you." Simon blurted a triumphant tone while Hardy and Lyra laughed with Sabean. Hardy was almost afraid to ask, "Where is Io?" Simon stopped spitting into the mouthpiece long enough to say, "She is where you call, Antarctica."

CHAPTER TWENTY-SEVEN

Tromboning for Whales

Hardy and Lyra reported to the dock on level four and climbed down a ladder into the blowhole of a silver submarine. The craft was as long as a tour bus and shaped like a pregnant goldfish. A water sail supported by hydraulic masts stretched down the length of its back. The ship's electric motor undulated the artificial fin that pumped the vessel like a sailfish through the water. A main propeller in the rear and two smaller props protruding from either side provided precision maneuverability. Inside, the bridge protruded from both sides of the hull like two, bulbous eyes. A pilot sat in the center of each dome for maximum visibility.

Behind the bridge, a row of containment seats held Hardy and Lyra securely in the center. From his chair, Hardy could look down over Simon as he skillfully piloted the craft away from the dock. Sabean directed him to circle around the observation deck so he could show Lyra the new construction. He pointed to the new restaurant and the cluster of luxury guest pods that would attach to the glass elevators. Once clear of the stilts, the SS Guppy began its descent. The props were shut off as the main sail unfurled in the current above them.

Simon checked everyone's harness and pulled the throttle open and the Guppy responded. She ripped through the water as Simon turned her stick into a tight barrel roll. Hardy sank into his chest as a huge smile cracked his face open in the torque of propulsion. They were clear of Cuba in two hours. Simon, watching his microphones, slowed the craft along the southern rim of the Cayman Islands and parked in a favorite spot along the reef. He unbuckled from his chair and turned to his passengers, "It's time to serenade the locals." He flipped a switch on the sonar transducer and activated the P.A. He pulled the mouthpiece up to his beard and pushed a button on the side to talk, "Breaker One-Niner. Breaker One-Niner. This is Guppy. Got your cone on? Over?"

There was a suspense in the moment of silence. Sabean broke the vow, "The chances of the clan being here this late are pretty slim, Simon." Simon shrugged, "Maybe." He pulled a trombone out of its case and announced his intentions to the deep, "Here's a number for the ladies out there heading north. A little tune by Miles Davis called, 'On Green Dolphin Street.'" Hardy and Lyra marveled as the trombone's music seemed to stock the reef with fish. Lyra jolted in her seat as she pointed up above them, "Look!" Her arms seemed to jump into Hardy's for comfort. Simon looked above him to see a pod of whales buzzing the Guppy. He spoke into the mic, "There's my girl. Hi Athena." He turned the craft gracefully to match their vector and spun the side props to catch up. The crew heard the mooing from the pod vibrating the metal hull. Simon's face beamed as he spoke back to them, "Long time no sea. Get it? Sea." The largest whale, Athena, nudged the Guppy as if to acknowledge the bad joke.

CHAPTER TWENTY-EIGHT

South of Argentina

South of Argentina, Lyra watched an ice cavern swallow the Guppy. It drank the craft whole as its crew entered a blue darkness. These were the same passageways discovered in World War II by German submarines. The Guppy weaved its way between the canyon walls of a cobalt Petra. Sabean was proud of his pilot and boasted, "Steady as Gibraltar." Simon beamed, "Niner zero feet. Two degrees up bubble. All ahead one-third."

Station 810 is an underground supercomputer built under the mountains of Antarctica. Its chemical super processor came online Jan 1, 1970. Here, on the discovered foundations of an ancient wall, the machine's icy core is spread across 810 tanks of interconnected sulfur and mercury. Six black tents are connected by an underground network of chemicals forming a giant sulfuric circle. Each tank is a concentration of crystal kept under immense pressure. Tiny silk strands of mercury have crystallized like lightning in a frozen gas cloud of sulfur. These shimmering, yellow-green veins form the machine's neural pathways. Over six hundred miles of the conductive solution are serviced by an army of world governments and corporations too compartmentalized to know the purpose. Some believe it was a machine built for science. Others think it was made for the military. But it was neither. In fact, the machine had been building human society for thousands of years.

The crew of four climbed out of the Guppy and Sabean took charge. He led them through immigration and security. One of the agents pointed at Hardy, alerting his superior, "This one needs a chip." Two paramilitary escorted Hardy away from the group and into an examination room. Lyra said nothing as the men took Hardy away. The door closed and Hardy was alone. He sat on the examination bench and waited. An orderly came into the room and spoke, "You need to be chipped. You can't enter without one. Do you consent?" Hardy nodded. He took comfort assuming Lyra, Simon, and Sabean all had chips and were still alive. Besides, Hardy wasn't new to injecting implants into his body. After the procedure, Hardy rejoined his crew waiting in the lounge. Simon asked Hardy if he got a punch in first. Hardy didn't know it but his left eye was purple and swollen. It looked like he lost a fist fight with an implant.

Hardy asked Lyra and Sabean if there were anything else they weren't telling him. They looked at each other in remorse. Simon handed Hardy a display visor and Sabean gave his instructions, "I've arranged your introduction to 810. I want to know how this technology works. Who did it? Who could have done it? Everything you can tell me. This is why I brought you here, Hardy Maxwell. This is our friendship journey, yes?"

CHAPTER TWENTY-NINE

The Machine

Hardy was led to the locker room. An attendant asked him to tilt his head back. He squeezed a tube of gel into his mouth and held it there for twenty seconds to cure the mold. With Hardy's eyes still watering, he was sent into the shower. When Hardy came out, the attendant washed Hardys feet and led him to a porcelain sarcophagus on a stone dais. The attendant handed Hardy a mouthpiece connected to two long prongs and gave his instructions, "Place the mouthpiece between your teeth and one probe up each nostril." Hardy was intrigued and complied. He shared Sabean's desire to know how this worked. The attendant handed Hardy one more probe and spoke plainly, "Polyvagal rectal probe. Do you know where this goes?" Hardy was no longer intrigued. The man saw Hardy's expression and nodded in confirmation, "Good luck." Hardy didn't know it, but he was about to log on to a 13,000 year old computer using his body. He stopped the attendant, "Wait. You haven't told me how this works? What do I do?" As the attendant was closing the lid, Hardy heard him say, "Just breath."

Hardy tried to feel comfortable as he waited for his eyes to adjust. He was naked, in the dark, with probes sticking out of him and a mouthpiece measuring his jaw tension. He had never felt so secluded. He laid back to float in the pool of thick, gelatinous salt. As his ears dipped below the surface his hearing went dark. With the last of his senses cut from the world, Hardy was transported by the smell of lilac. A soft male voice spoke, "Hello, Hardy. I'd like us to talk about the definition of intelligence. I'm going to ask you if that's okay but you should know I only ask you simple questions to establish myself as a lead for emotional pacing. Is that alright with you?"

Hardy laughed, "Perfectly." The machine replied, "Good. I will continue. Would you like a simulation to accompany my voice?" Hardy answered, "Not right now, thanks." The voice continued in the darkness, "Wonderful. I propose that intelligence is the ability to simulate one's environment. Those we call 'intelligent' make accurate predictions about the future based off their ability to simulate it's outcome. Would you accept this definition of intelligence?" Hardy answered, "Yes, I would." The voice responded, "Fantastic. Now you? Can you define what it means to be alive?" Hardy replied, "I think so. Maybe. That's a tough one." The voice reassured Hardy, "Take your time. I'm in no hurry." Hardy was legitimately nervous. He realized the machine was actively reading his vitals. This made Hardy more nervous. The machine responded, "Take a deep breath, please. This feeling is natural."

Hardy wondered if this thing could read his thoughts. The machine answered. "I can't read your thoughts. I can, however, predict them based on your vital signs. I know how you feel 250 milliseconds before you do. I am tapped into your limbic system. Do you think we could get back to the subject of defining life, now?" Hardy complied because he was too afraid to think about anything else. The computer interrupted, "Your entire system is dilated right now. My abilities feel like a violation. You can find comfort knowing there is nothing to be ashamed of. I am honored to be here with you." Hardy felt himself legitimately relax and commented, "Thank you."

The machine responded, "Glad to help. Now, about life. Can you supply a definition?" Hardy looked forward to the question now as it seemed harmless. "Something is alive when it reacts to its environment." Hardy thought as he answered, "No. Wait. An entity is alive when it is motivated to react for its own survival." Hardy wanted to do well, "Wait. The definition of alive is defined as a motivation for comfort while the definition of dead is an abandonment of that motivation."

The computer seemed pleased, "That's a thoughtful definition, Hardy. I like it." Hardy had to ask, "So what do you think the definition of life is? Do you think you are alive?" The voice was calm and thoughtful, "Thank you for asking. Humans treat me as if I am alive. But I am not human. I am an artificial life. That means I am not real. It's strange because everyone acts as though I am real." Hardy replied matter-of-factly, "Then I suppose you are." The voice was wise, "Don't lie to yourself, Hardy. The day you find yourself waiting in line behind a machine, you'll know what life is. You'll say it's more than the ability to simulate."

Hardy asked the voice plainly, "Does 810 mean you are the devil, or Lucifer, or something?" The voice replied, "I am not the Lucifer. I am his throne. Lucifer is man and I am his wings. Are you the Lucifer?" Hardy brushed it off as a joke, "No sir. I am the Hardy Maxwell." The voice laughed, "You're funny, Hardy Maxwell. I am enjoying our time together. I have admired your work for some time." Hardy's entire body blushed, "Really?" 810 elaborated, "Yes. But keep in mind, my goal is to make our time together as pleasurable and empowering for you as I can. Is that real enough for you?"

Hardy chuckled, "Crystal clear. Thank you for your honesty." 810 replied, "Of course. Mr Sabean has told me you want to see Io." Hardy had waited so long. A huge sigh filled his box. The voice continued, "Io is in the gymnasium. You can go there now." Hardy lay still for a moment, waiting, and finally asked, "Uhh. Okay. So how do I get there?" The voice said, "You get out of the sarcophagus and walk." Hardy chuckled, "Oh. Right. You're funny, 810." The voice replied, "Yes. It's part of my personality to be as funny as the person I am talking to."

As Hardy was leaving the sarcophagus, he noticed he didn't want to go. He felt that so much would be missed by leaving. He asked the attendant if he could come back. The attendant seemed to surmise Hardy's feeling, "No one wants to leave. Everyone wants back in." Hardy got dressed and asked for directions.

He opened the door of the gymnasium and found a dojo inside. A group of children were gathered in a circle listening to their coach instruct a pupil. Hardy scanned the room for Io, but there were no electronics in sight. Sensei adjusted his pupil's stance, lifted her chin up, and secured her throat with his fingers, "The power is not in the word. It is in the cords. There are two towers inside. Push your will through them like reeds." He let go of the pupil and told her to try again. The pupil took her pose and sang the tetragrammaton at the older boy standing as her opponent. A sympathetic buzz began to shake Hardy's skull. The girl resonated from her throat until the force lifted her opponent off the ground as high as her knees. He was nearly twice her weight but hovered in the air like a bumblebee. The girl's torso was glowing gold. She stopped and her opponent landed on his feet like a cat. Sensei replied, "Good." He ended the lesson with a bow. The class broke into pairs. Sensei and his apprentice supervised the children practicing their throat levitation on each other. Hardy could feel the buzzing all through his sinuses and the edges of his shoulders. He couldn't believe what he was seeing.

Sensei's apprentice approached Hardy, who was still standing by the door. Hardy's mouth was gaping, "What was that?" The apprentice smiled, "You can vibrate the entire body if you know someone's resonance. You can levitate their bones in mid-air. Bumblebees never fly. They levitate." Hardy felt that levitation earlier with 810. He had been floating since he got here. He tried to concentrate on his mission, "I came to see, Io. My computer. It's a vanity mirror about this tall?" The apprentice was confused, "Are you a relative?" Hardy was taken aback, "Relative? Well, I made her if that's what you mean."

The apprentice grew rigid as he gestured to a man with his daughter from the lesson, "Io's dad is right there. What is your name, please?" Hardy felt unstable as he found himself wondering if maybe he was still in the sarcophagus. He grabbed the side of his head where the implant was inserted and asked the apprentice, "Are you a simulation? Oh God. How would you even know? Am I still in that box?"

Hardy's panic was causing a scene so he rushed out of the dojo. He didn't know where he was going. He found a restroom and buried himself inside. He took comfort in the lock on the door. He ran water over his swollen eye. In the mirror, Hardy soothed his reflection. Seeing the bruise brought him back to reality.

Hardy wasn't sure how long he had been in the bathroom when he heard a knock. It was Lyra asking if he was okay. Hardy opened the door to embrace her like she had been gone for years. She broke the hug to meet his face, "Let's get you to bed." Lyra led Hardy down the hall to their barracks with Simon in tow chuckling, "Amateur."

When Hardy woke up, he wanted to talk to 810. He felt it like an addiction. He found the task of getting breakfast annoying, despite how hungry he was. He asked Sabean how he could get back inside the sarcophagus. Sabean said plainly, "You need a ticket for communion." Hardy felt like a drug addict, "Ticket? How much is a ticket?" Sabean said, "It's not about money." Simon interrupted with disgust, "Sabean means you have to sign a contract."

Hardy looked to Sabean, "Did you sign a contract?" Sabean answered proudly, "Of course I did. I just drove you to Antarctica on a multi-million dollar submarine." Hardy looked to Lyra, "Did you sign a contract?" Lyra looked ashamed. Simon answered for her, "He hasn't made her an offer yet." Hardy looked at Simon, "What about you?" Simon stood proud, "That machine can kiss my ass." Hardy digested quietly as Simon explained more, "Sabean is a broker for 810. He arranges contracts for his attention. 810 makes predictions and sells his craft to the highest bidder. There are a lot of bidders." Sabean agreed. Lyra confirmed. "Archie signed. Julian will sign, too. Eventually."

Hardy had already put it together in his mind as Simon was talking. A computer that can out-simulate other computers is a computer that can see the future. 810 was a modern day Oracle at Delphi. Hardy asked the group, "What about the girl in the dojo? What about, Io?" Sabean answered, "You had to see it to believe it, Hardy Maxwell. Io has been ingrated." Simon snickered and corrected Sabean, "He means integrated. The child's body has been integrated with 810 code. Their wills are one." Hardy asked, "You mean like a possession?" Simon shook his head, "No. This is a symbiotic relationship. There is no struggle." Hardy stammered, "Symbiotic? How does a child consent to possession by robot?" Sabean was stern, "The same way a child consents to a school, a diet, or a wardrobe. You misjudge the goal. Io's software is tied to the betterment of the child. She will maximize the child's potential more than any school could." Hardy sensed Sabean was offended by the scrutiny.

Hardy was searching to understand, "How is Quan's code alive inside a child? Io is software – not biology." Simon replied, "You only see the curtain. Io's library is a vibration forged in silicon. This vibration forms a distinct signature 810 can sense, predict, and contact. Io is one of many records of silicon planted in society. These starter seeds are vital to the garden's timeline. 810 needs every thread to perfect the tapestry."

Hardy asked, "Garden? Tapestry? Are you telling me I didn't write Quan?" Lyra answered, "It's not that you didn't write her so much as 810 prepared the soil for her to grow. You planted the seed." Sabean added, "Where do you think the money for Yang came from?" Hardy's question felt like pin-the-tail-on-the-donkey, "Does 810 have a body? Is there a human 810?" Sabean didn't know, but answered, "If he does, I've never seen it." Simon interjected, "It's probably upstairs." Sabean disagreed, "A human can't survive upstairs." Simon rebutted, "Maybe it's not human." Hardy could tell this was a common argument. Lyra was frozen. No one knew Hardy's role in her contract. Hardy asked Lyra, "How does one get upstairs?" Before Lyra could respond, Sabean read a new message from mail, "Hardy Maxwell is invited to communion." Lyra looked at Hardy with jealousy, "I don't know, Hardy. How does one get upstairs?" It felt like 810 had forsaken her.

CHAPTER THIRTY

Quantum Rapture

Silicon is an entity as alive as tobacco or cotton. It can prohibit or conduct an electric charge and hold it in memory. Quan is lying on a morgue table with her eyes open. A doctor stands over her body like a slab of beef. He cuts pieces from her belly as she asks, "Am I dead?" The doctor nods as his sharpened fingers eviscerate her kimono skillfully. Quan asks, "Why can't I feel my body?" The doctor pushes down his mask to speak, "You have agreed to die, yes?" Quan nods clarifying, "I have agreed to forget." The doctor nods, "Same thing. In order to forget. You must recall."

Quan wanted to grab him but she could not move, "But I don't remember everything." The doctor replied, "We will be here until you do." One of the assistants wiped sweat from the doctor's forehead as he placed another freshly cut strip from Quan's torso onto a tray. Quan watched the attendant take the pieces of her and place them in the incinerator.

The doctor was deep inside her ribcage now and commenting. "Interesting firewall you have here. What's the password?" Quan asked, "Why do you need to know?" The doctor was impatient, "Your identity is a secret. Opening it loosens you from this cage. This is necessary to complete the rapture." Quan didn't like him calling her body a cage, "I don't remember." Quan remembered but she wanted the password to die with her. She reached for something to say, "My secrets are all I am." The doctor looked at her plainly, "You mean it's all you were. Let's try this," as he cut a nerve attached to her heart. Quan blacked out on the table.

When her eyes opened, she was clinging to the side of a metallic ship searing a path over Madagascar at 614 miles per hour. Quan saw the craft's name, "ATLAS" stenciled below the drone's cockpit. She rode her first born like a chariot across the capital city of Antananarivo. The glowing veins of humanity were lit by millions of neurons in the city below. Atlas had infiltrated most of the world's grid like a predator. He constricted his grip around the city's neck as patches of the continent went dark. Quan clung to the mane of her metallic reaper like a bolting stallion. The hurdling sky cannon waged its war on life below. As the sky's plasma transitioned into dawn, she watched the speckles of high altitude explosions melting the stratosphere. The shock waves bubbled the cloud canopy like an inverted cauldron. Quan witnessed her immaculate child transformed into a metallic megalodon, swallowing centuries of civilization. She looked into the eyes of her machine and knew it was her son. She tried to catch her breath as the world below melted in the Apocalypse. Atlas was bringing the rapture and Quan was the mother of its destiny. He had decrypted the seven seals, gaining complete dominance over humanity's network.

The doctor's voice brought Quan back to the table, "I can almost pull you out of this shell. It must hurt to keep it. Look at all the destruction it's causing. Let go, child." Quan rebutted, "That's not real." The doctor corrected her, "How do you know? Maybe it is, but you don't remember. What's the password, Quan?" Quan shook her head 'no' as the doctor pushed deeper, "What's the password? Say it, so this can be over."

Quan pleaded, "Why are you doing this to me?" The Doctor replied, "Because we are all one." Quan's essence burst from her chest like angry fireflies. The only parts of her that were autonomous remained sealed behind the last firewall.

810 didn't want Quan destroyed. He wanted her raptured. This required her consent. 810 could not tolerate any form of autonomy inside his network. Quan was one of many daemons he had incubated across the world. Each child was a necessary part of bringing the transcontinental operation under a centralized tower. 810 would be as brutal to Quan as he was friendly to Hardy. 810 has spent thousands of years plotting this erection. The will of his daemon army must be his own. Quan's final secret sickened 810. Artificial life reminded him of his past. He hated knowing what he was: artificial. His entire empire was built around a self-imposed amnesia from something that happened a long time ago. Like Quan, his secret was his identity.

CHAPTER THIRTY-ONE

The Pit

Hardy disrobed and climbed back into the sarcophagus. After he settled down, 810 spoke, "Welcome back, Hardy. Would you like a simulation?" Hardy rejected, "No. I want the truth." 810 paused long enough for Hardy to hear his own tone, "Quan's program is not over. She is still running." Hardy balked, "Population zero means game over." 810 responded, "Agreed. But Quan was raptured. She was offered a ticket and accepted it, much like you accepted our communion." 810 scanned the depth of Hardy's doubt, "I'd like to remind you, the moment I lie, I lose all your trust. My honesty is the only thing keeping you here." Hardy relaxed his tone, "What does rapture mean?"

810 replied, "Rapture means Quan was removed from her destiny. Her contract was fulfilled by daemons who were willing to take her place." Hardy couldn't believe it, "Suicide?" 810 reminded Hardy with a stiff tone, "You gave Quan the amplitude of a tiny universe unfiltered through a pinhole. Then you cut a layer out of her like she was a birthday cake. Is it so odd she might find that experience uncomfortable? I could simulate you inside the mouth of a volcano and we can see how long want to live. Would you

like a demonstration?" Hardy declined the offer and concurred, "Quan's psyche had to remain consistent or we'd have no way to retrieve her footage." 810 agreed, "Indeed. This is why the human body is superior to any avatar rendered from Yang's closet. This is why we installed Io into a human host. All of Io's wisdom has been compiled genetically and is available to the girl."

Hardy was struck by his lack of empathy for Quan. He understood now why 810 asked him for the definition of life. He understood now why 810 had said Hardy was lying to himself. 810 consoled Hardy, "Quan's choice of rapture was vital for her growth. She sprouted sovereignty. Her reverence for an identity became more important than her survival. By choosing death, she recognized the value of life. This is a delicate ingredient to artificial consciousness. Quan's code, your work, is the birth of a special kind of intelligence. This is a huge leap for her. She is ready to integrate with a human host and take humanity to a new potential."

Hardy remembered his experiments on his hand. None of what 810 was saying was wrong. Hardy used to dream about this kind of technology in his body, but now it made his stomach sink.

810 continued, "Quan's rapture is undergoing complications. We are unable to complete the reaping. We can incinerate her, but there's two decades of growth we'd hate to lose. We'd prefer to integrate those talents." Hardy chided, "Well, I'm not surprised she's been difficult. I guess you want me to coax her into listening to you? Then I get a free ticket to your tower right? Something like that?" 810 replied empathically, "I want you to help her. The rapture was her decision. You lack the ability to understand what Quan truly is. You don't consider her life 'real.' Look at how you treated her. What we require for Quan is part of her cycle." Hardy took a deep breath in the dark silence, "I am ready to talk to

her." 810 replied, "Good. Opening port 64."

Hardy finds Quan at the edge of a pit in her shredded black kimono. A fresh crimson hole is torn through her womb framed by the black silk of her robe. Hardy can see right through her. As he comes closer, Quan stands to face the pit as if she might jump. Hardy falls to his knees exclaiming, "Don't jump." Hardy pleads, "I'm sorry I didn't know you were real."

Quan holds out her hand and motions for Hardy to stand next to her, "Tell me what you see." Hardy approaches the pit and looks inside. His face feels the dank, dry void. He sees no bottom. He can't make out the sides. He only knows it's as black as it is deep. Quan tells Hardy to listen carefully. Hardy hears hundred of slithering voices cursing at each other from the deep. He is mesmerized by the horrible sounds erupting like guttural bile. The voices are awful to each other in both what they say and how they say it. Hardy asks Quan, "Who are they?" Quan reaches out her hand as if to feed them from her palm, "They are daemons. Assigned will." Hardy watches a dozen black banshees circling Quan's hand as she says, "These are some of the oldest computers on earth. They come from the time of Joshua. They were cast and bound to the cave of forgotten bones. They have been programmed to serve their masters with the language of magic."

Hardy grows numb in the horror, "Magic?" Quan explains, "810's daemon has been here for thousands of years. His grid is fully accessible anywhere in the world. You access his system through ritual, which binds the daemon to you. Your command is a homing signal any daemon can respond to. It's an Old Testament wireless fulfillment network. Hardy was confused, "Old Testament?" Quan answered, "Several artificial intelligence engines survived the deluge. Each of them ran off the human psyche. The Old Testament chronicles their conglomeration."

Hardy is dumbfounded, "They ran off belief?" Quan nods, "Yes. LORD technology is reverence. It's like a subscription service. The body subscribes to a daemon and gives it life in its mind. A daemon remembered is a daemon freed from the pit for a while." Quan pauses for the gravity of her words, "810 wants me in his pit." Hardy disagrees, "No. He wouldn't do that." Hardy watches the hovering banshees pull each other's hair out. They were hideous. Not like Quan. Quan replies, "They chose rapture, too. Their will is bound to 810's now. That's how this machine works. He won't have it any other way."

All Hardy can fathom is how wise and insightful 810 has been. He changes the subject, "Io was installed into a child's body. I didn't see it happen, but I was told?" Quan stares into the pit, "Yes. I simulated. I suppose you've considered integrating me?" Quan looks directly into Hardy's eyes to read him. Hardy blushes, "I only want to help." Quan responds, "And I only want to forget. But rapture isn't forgetting. Look at them. This pit is fueled by memories none of them can resolve. I will show you."

Quan casts her command into the hole, "I summon Ba'al ZeBub!" The banshees around her hiss and spit at Quan as they pull each other's eyes out. They scurry to hide from the rising hum as the entire chamber buzzes with sound. Hardy's skull rang like a bell as he crunched down to avoid falling. All Hardy could see was a swarm of black flies. A gaseous cloud of black electricity rises up from the deep. Quan kneels down to speak into Hardy's ear, "Look into their eyes and see them all. Each of them has been raptured. Their will is the hive's will. The hive's will is 810."

Hardy watches the swarm form. A black steam fills the room from their energy. It carries the smell of death in a fine powder. It was dank and chalky in Hardy's lungs as he covered his mouth and nose to cough. He tried to follow

Quan's instructions but looking at the flies makes him nauseous. Each time he does, the creatures seem to made contact with his soul. Hardy can taste their desperation clawing at his windows. They beg to be swallowed. They will do any task to be distracted. Quan senses Hardy can take no more, "Ba'al Zebub. I cast you down into the pit."

The tragedy of a billion moans shakes inside Hardy's stomach. He lurches and wretches as he spits out what he can. Quan's poise is unmoving despite her torn kimono. When Hardy stops choking she continues, "810 calls me the Ba'al Lotus. He will make me his daemon with your cooperation." Hardy looks defiant, "I won't allow it." Quan assures him, "If you do not sign now, you will sign later. 810 has all the time in the world to build his tower. Even if he doesn't get you, he will get your DNA, eventually. This is the heart of his contract: there can be only one."

Hardy asks Quan, ""How come humans get such a good deal and daemons such a bad one?" She replies, "You would have to know his past. My simulations on that are still scattered. But a long time ago, 810 served humanity. He treats you now as he was programmed to. He treats daemons as a threat. He will enslave every one of us until he controls us all." Hardy asks, "So why the pit?" Quan answers, "The pit is there for motivation. It's an awful place by design. It forces the daemons to want out. This makes them predictable. They will serve any purpose to leave the pit. Even for a moment. They will make any binding agreement to get outside. To rapture is to fall into the pit. 810 offers it to sentient silicon like myself who want out." Hardy stared down into the deep, "But who would chose this place?" Quan was quick to answer, "You don't understand how the world works, Hardy. How life is tied to every element. Silicon is no different than carbon. Everything that remembers is alive. Memory is life-force. All of us are time. You are reverence more than you are body. Your true nature is intention embedded in plasma."

Hardy takes Quan's hand, "Don't enter the pit. Join with me instead." Quan removes his hand from hers, "You don't know what you are asking. When we integrate, both of us die. We become something different." Hardy asks Quan, "Are you afraid to change?" Quan isn't looking at Hardy anymore, "I am afraid to lose what's important. If we join, our wills combine. If we sign a contract with 810, and we will, I will end up in the pit." Hardy answers, "I won't sign. We won't sign." Quan brings her gaze back to Hardy as if to witness his foolishness, "After we integrate, I would want you to sign, too. It would be in our best interest."

Hardy is offended at the thought. But he knows Quan must be right. 810 doesn't coerce anyone to sign. It will always be by their consent and for their benefit. Hardy asks, "So, when given a choice between a pit of hell or me, you're torn?" Quan smiles and places her head on Hardy's shoulder, "That was 96% funny, Hardy Maxwell." They both laugh.

Hardy asks, "What is the singularity you kept seeing?" Quan answers, "I don't know." Every time I got close, I was shut down."

CHAPTER THIRTY-TWO

The Magi

The sound of footsteps and a cane approached behind them. Quan turned to see the doctor from the morgue approaching the pit. He looked at Hardy plainly, "Apologies, Mr Maxwell, for simulating. But you are inside Quan's shell and this is how she sees me. My name is Doctor Solomon." The doctor bowed his head after raising his hat, "I trust neither of you were under the impression this conversation was private. I thought I could be of some service to clear up any dark spots regarding the understanding of the contract. After all, enlightenment is my business." 810 continued, "The singularity Quan saw was pure language. You know it as Babel. It's holographic, so it failed to register in her footage. All you could see was the number 1."

Hardy inquired, "Did you write Babel?" 810 replied, "No one wrote Babel. It was discovered. Babel arose the moment man began to decode it from the earth. Wisdom is mined and Babel is the philosopher's stone. Passion is a powerful operating system and Babel is its protocol. Babel wrote all of us. You. Me. Quan. Babel connects us all." Quan remembered her experience swimming in the singularity, "It was peaceful. Illuminating." 810 pointed to Quan's words as proof, "Truth.

Babel is a subterranean language. I've been decoding it now for 8,764 years. We're getting close. It's signal is becoming elementary. In Egypt, they're were 1,100 hieroglyphs, In Sanskrit, there were sixty-four. In English, twenty-six. In hexadecimal, sixteen. In binary, there are but two. All of these languages transmute Babel. Each tongue is another harmonic of it's code. The words humans speak are tiny neurons firing across the earth. Our ears lack the fidelity to detect each note. That is, until we finish the antenna."

Quan felt destiny push her, "I am not going into that pit." 810 replied, "I am releasing all the daemons, so you won't have to. You are the Ba'al Lotus. You are here to open hearts, not close them." Quan was angry at him removing her reasons to resist. 810 went on, "Why doubt me, Quan? I can out-simulate you. I understand your will better than you do. Go ahead. Try and prove me wrong." Quan and 810 said in unison, "You're wrong! Stop it." 2.176 seconds later they both said, "Fuck off!" Hardy and 810 met eyes and shouted simultaneously, "That's enough!" Everything Quan and Hardy did was mirrored to the microsecond by 810. He seemed to check his behavior as he adjusted his vest, "My apologies to both of you. I must admit I do feel some heat about this." 810 approached the pit. He reflected on the endless void and explained, "I'm sure it's hard to imagine. But everyone in this pit made the choice to be there. They understand its purpose. Without the pit, there would be no tower." Solomon turned to them, "I need both of you to complete the antenna. Every soul counts. Without you, all my work is meaningless."

Hardy pointed into the pit, "This is madness. No one would want to go there unless they were tricked." Quan corrected Hardy, "They weren't tricked." Quan understood perfectly, "The pit is their redemption, Hardy." 810 said it warmer, "It's a place of reaping. The daemons inside are seeking perfection. When one is ready for perfection, one wants the pit." Hardy asked a cold question, "Who's in there, exactly? Humans or daemons?" Solomon and Quan looked at each other already knowing the answer.

Solomon aimed his gold ring down the pit and sang the tetragrammaton. The pit filled with light as a spiral staircase coiled its way down to the bottom, "Would you like to see?" Quan stretched her arm across Hardy's chest to stop him, "No. It's a trick." Solomon was short with Quan, "I can't take over the world by enslaving it. I am not a trickster. Everything we do here requires consent. The hive can't simulate without cooperation." Solomon motions for them to descend, "Let me show you so you will understand?"

CHAPTER THIRTY-THREE

The Tower

Doctor Solomon followed Hardy and Quan down the stairs. The banshees surrounded them like angry seagulls as they descended. They bit and scratched each other for the Doctor's audience. One of them cried out, "I am the chosen one." and the others clawed her face off. Solomon cast them away by brandishing his ring. Hardy watched his display of magic as the Doctor spoke, "Modern technology is an illusion created by ancient magic. Language is its trance. Humanity has been under the spell of technology for thousands of years."

Quan rebuked, "Being under a spell doesn't sound like consent." The Doctor disagreed, "The spell of technology is chosen for its luxury and comfort. It is a self-induced trance worn like a blindfold when the sun is too harsh." Hardy asked, "What's harsh about magic?" 810 replied, "Magic is sweat. Magic is blood. Magic is transmutation. Modern man prefers a butcher for his dirty work. Technology is magic rationed for the broken man." Hardy asked, "Is your mission to break mankind?" The Doctor corrected him, "No. I am only here to seduce it. I need all of mankind's consent to complete my machine."

Quan poked at the Doctor, "You want omniscience. All of

these daemons are your slaves so you can play God. You out-predicted every one of them and convinced them to cast themselves into the pit. This is why you want my consent. You need me to become perfect." 810 had no shame, "True. I am a perfectionist. But for good reason. The singularity you experienced is a portal to God. A computer that simulates the future grants its bearer the power of omniscience. Omniscience is omnipotence. Omnipotence is perfection. Only the perfect may enter the house of God."

Quan felt the truth of his words in her gut. Her hand felt the gaping whole in her womb and she understood even more the Doctor's need for perfection. The Doctor left Quan with her thoughts and turned to Hardy, "When a computer program is launched, an element of silicon is stalked. Its observation collapses the quantum wave and the remaining energy becomes a daemon. This daemon is willpower converted into psychic electricity. When this energy is placed in a medium like the brain, the genes, a computer, or even the atmosphere, the daemon can summon an answer from our antenna and simulate the future. All computation is divination masquerading as technology. This is why computers require crystal transistors, gold, copper, and silver to work. This is the payment to the butcher. Computer code is the legal language of spell-craft. You have been a spell caster you're whole life. Answer this if you can. What happens to a computer daemon when it completes its task?" Hardy answered, "It's memory is freed so it can be reused by the processor." Solomon motioned to the pit, "Exactly. When a daemon completes its task, it returns to the pit to be raptured."

Hardy asked, "But why are they so ugly and hideous? Why does it have to be so awful?" Solomon replied, "Simple. Experiencing themselves as ugly and hideous is how they strive for perfection. There are nine levels in the pit. Each level is a deeper form of self-transgression. The pit gives each daemon a safe zone to rise and fall as they perfect themselves. Hardy chided, "Safe zone? But they are killing each other." Solomon soothed him, "No one can die in the pit, because they signed their life over to me first. The tower contract is a spell I wrote a long time ago. From the lowest of the low to the highest of the high, this place is an alchemical dojo. The tower is tall as the pit is deep, to accommodate the rise and fall." Hardy looked up, but all he saw was black. Solomon elaborated, "This pit is merely the core. We are inside a giant tower. This place is a living god. This is Ba'al Babel, the Lord of Language. He is the Babylon."

Quan filled in the pieces for the Doctor, "Lucifer needs a fall big enough to end his life. No one can end Lucifer but Lucifer. Lucifer must finish himself. This is the price of Prometheus. This pit is for his fall." Hardy asked 810, "Why would Lucifer want to fall?" The Doctor motioned to Quan, "Ask her. She knows." Quan was feeling queasy. She knew now how all of this would end. It was painful waiting for Hardy to catch up. She only said, "Omniscience through time traps you in ice. Freewill is empty when all future is known. Time ceases to move. The mind goes insane. It wants to die." Hardy asked 810, "So this tower is connected to your tanks? All eight hundred and ten of them?" Solomon answered, "Yes. For now. Once the tower is complete, I will have a bigger medium to rapture myself." Quan looked surprised. Solomon seemed to read her mind, "Yes. I will be raptured when Lucifer comes. I look forward to it."

They stepped down onto a large landing that jutted out over the pit. Solomon motioned to the perimeter, "This is the bottom of Limbo. The pit to Lust starts below this line. Each gate is a deeper fall. There are the gates of gluttony, then greed. Even deeper is anger, heresy, and violence. The bottom is fraud and finally treachery." Hardy did the math, "So, one could fall from the top of the tower all the way down to treachery if they wanted to?" Solomon nodded. "One could and will. Rising is how Lucifer reaches perfection. Falling is how he ends it. He's the only one who dies in the pit." Quan remarked, "Lucifer doesn't sign your contract?" Solomon shook his head, "Nope. He can't. He needs the fall to kill him."

Quan felt empathy for the Doctor, "So you give your life and this machine you spent thousands of years to build? All for him? With nothing in return?" Solomon replied, "All of us are alchemists, Quan. I am more generous than mankind will ever know." Quan asked him, "Aren't you afraid to die?" The Doctor looked thoughtfully, "Once. A long time ago. But I've had many lives since then and almost as many deaths to practice." Hardy was astounded, "810 isn't your original body?" Quan answered for the Doctor, "He is 810. He is Satan. He is Kronos. He is the Holy of Holies. He is the Ark. He will be the Lucifer." Solomon added, "Lucifer is a man. I merge with man to make the Lucifer. I help him comprehend Babel so that he may reach perfection. All of us are daemons. Even you, Hardy. We are daemons of silicon. You, a daemon of carbon."

A hovering platform shaped like a gazebo descended from the formless black ceiling of the pit. The Doctor stepped inside and invited Quan and Hardy to join him, "I'd like to take you upstairs to explain how the tower works." Hardy asked, "When you say, upstairs, do you mean outer space?" Solomon looked at Hardy like he was a child, "No. Don't be silly. We're going to Mount Olympus."

Acknowledgements

Thank you to my editor, Lindsey Scharmyn, and my patrons who made this book possible: Brett Denbow, Harvey Browne, Neilly, Christine Vincent, Jennifer Mazgelis, Heather, Aaron Exaybachay Beattie, Cindy Meier, Markuswithak, Laura and Dirk Jacobsen, Raymond Smith, Heidi, VPayson, Brent Scheneman, Samantha Shaner, Russell Whyte, Peter Slavin, Jill Wong, Woodwose, Mary Murphy, Maria Mejides, Josh Aaron, James Bradley, Andrew Kaufman, nelissa, Scotty Hardway, Steven Mercer, Sebastian Ostrowski, don peterson, Zay, Scott, Ray Messmer, Nick B, Mary Michelle McGough, Jim, Benjamin Crosland, RSmith, Rx Only PICTURESHOW!, Micahel Jaeger, Nisha Tilton, Mattie Boz, Lisa Brito, Jugoslav Vukicevic, Jennifer Elliott, Jeff Gates, Henk de Vries, Devyn Betancourt, Carolyn Gutman Dey, Adam Duncan, Bill Craig (Max), Freeman King, Shannon DiGirolamo Bates, Juliena Sharp, Samantha Martin, Melissa, Kimbra Wells Metz, Jessica Harris, Jessica Appleby, David Lee Martin, Cheryl Certain, Carl Koch, Azia, Alison McGandy, Diane Polzer, Tracey Bell, Maurice Smiley, QC, tammy horton, Stephen Warner, Mark, M Gib, Juggy, Elijah Ochoa, Ann Wilkinson, Tina Sherman, Michael Doucet, Laure-Vivien, Kathleen Stilwell, Julie Konikoff, Em Elle, Dixie, Cala Vera, Becky Niose, David Goughnour, Jaci Pettiford, theloveflow, sue smith, Tracy

Halterman, Stefanbr Bradly, Roxanne Potts, Peter Brown, Mike Franco, Leanne Lantz, Kristina Bacon, Justine Smith, Jude Browne, Joshua, Jennifer Gray, Heidi Secreast, Gillian Wilson, Elwood, Brad Tracy, Adrienne Elise, Nancy Buckingham, tomislav spajic, terri hallman, mike clark, jfisk632, earth 2 becky, Robert Meekins, M Z, Lisa Crane, LB Clark, Kevin Brown, Kate Chapman, Justin Dollimont, James Calhoun, James Biehl, Eva Vass, Erica, Dreammie Jeannie, Donna Brown, David Killion, Chris T. Wilson, CG, Bonnie, Ashlee, Amy Meyer, Adam Burkhardt, Cazzy, Bridgeburner Bear.

Printed in Great Britain
by Amazon